Ruby Red and Dead

A JULIA GREENE TRAVEL MYSTERY

Linda Clayton

This book is fiction. All characters, events, and organizations portrayed in this novel are the product of the author's imagination or are used fictitiously. Any resemblance to actual persons—living or dead—is entirely coincidental.

For information, email Cozy Cat Press at:
cozycatpress@gmail.com
or visit our website at:
www.cozycatpress.com

ISBN: 978-1-952579-27-1

Printed in the United States of America

10 9 8 7 6 5 4 3 2 1

To Dan and Maria

Chapter 1

The high-pitched, shrill scream pierces the soft Moroccan afternoon air and silences even the birds in the palm trees. Malika Kettani drops the silver teapot she holds poised over my cup, and it clatters to the ground, bounces once and falls into the pool.

A wailing woman wearing a djellaba and a headscarf runs across the lawn in bare feet. She skids to a stop in front of us, wide-eyed and out of breath. "You must come, madam. *Vite! Il est mort.* He is dead!"

Malika jumps to her feet and takes the quivering woman's hands in hers. "Who is dead? What are you talking about? Pull yourself together, Imane, and tell me."

The woman stares at Mal, terror in her huge eyes. "Abdul! It is Abdul. He is on the driveway. It is so awful. You come now."

Malika, or Mal, as we call her, Olivia Duncan, my best friend, and I run after the wailing woman until we reach a small gathering of people huddled together. Next to them is a body on the ground. I take one look and gag. There's an enormous puddle of blood on the driveway and a gaping, bloody slash in the man's neck.

I've seen dead bodies before but never one that has been freshly murdered or with so much blood. And it has to be murder because it's difficult to slash your throat accidentally. I have to clamp my hand over my mouth to prevent the contents of my stomach from spilling out.

Mal's face is the color of paste. "That's Abdul, He was Peter's driver. He was a wonderful person. How could this happen?"

This remark makes the little huddle of four older women wail even louder. They cling to each other and look devastated. Kadem Kettani, Mal's father-in-law, strides across the lawn, and the little group silently fades away. He looks down at the dead man and shakes his head.

"He was attacked in the street. Probably thugs looking for money. Someone will come for him soon. Bring your guests back in the house, Malika. This isn't something they should see."

I want to protest that this seems awfully cold. Shouldn't we stay here until help comes? But M. Kettani doesn't look like he's in the mood to be challenged. The three of us trudge dutifully after him, through the magnificent garden and into the palatial, 14,000-square-foot home in a fancy suburb of Marrakech. Mal leads us into a room big enough to host the Super Bowl which is filled with red velvet furniture, heavy silk drapes, and vases full of gorgeous flowers. She plops down on a couch and buries her face in her hands.

"It just keeps getting worse and worse. I'm so glad you guys are here. You have no idea."

No, we can't possibly have an idea because Olivia and I landed in Morocco this morning, and I'm still wearing the clothes I put on thirty-six hours ago at my house is Wake Forest, North Carolina. And my head is throbbing because I unwisely stayed awake all night drinking wine and talking to a fellow passenger as we crossed the Atlantic.

My name is Julia Greene, and Olivia and I own Little Bites, a bakery and lunchroom in Wake Forest, North Carolina. We're also purveyors of delicious gourmet sauces, jams and jellies. We sell a tomato-bacon butter that will knock your socks off. Also several kinds of pickles, and once a week we offer freshly baked, scrumptious profiteroles and our bestselling item—key lime pie—the reason Olivia and I are on this trip.

Malika and Peter Kettani, old friends from my days at UNC, used to be regular customers at Little Bites. Malika loved our warm, sweet pastries and was particularly fond of my pies. She and her husband recently moved from Chapel Hill to their new home in Marrakech and are planning to have a big party to celebrate their seventh anniversary, and they want to serve delicious, delectable key lime pie.

When Malika, or Mal, as we call her, said she absolutely had to have some for her party, I tried to mentally calculate how I could ship a large quantity of highly perishable pie to Africa without guaranteeing the unlucky recipients a lethal case of e-coli or a container full of melted sticky goo. I had to tell her it couldn't be done. My friend, however, doesn't take no for an answer. She solved the problem by sending first class plane tickets to Olivia and me and promising I would have full access to her kitchen and all the necessary ingredients.

So here we are. A few hours ago we were flying across the Atlantic dreaming about an exotic vacation and now a man has been killed and our good friend is obviously upset about something.

I put my arms around her and say, "You sure look unhappy. Is something wrong, other than the unfortunate man on the driveway? I certainly don't want to pry, but is there anything we can do to help? Do you want to talk about it?" We'd often stayed up late talking when we were students at UNC. In those days we had no secrets. If we had a problem, we spilled it.

Malika shakes her head. "Y'all just landed in Morocco, and here I am telling you my troubles." She tries to smile, but it doesn't quite reach her eyes. "It's been a bit of a mess since we arrived here. I mean, Peter's father has been lovely to us, and I'm trying hard to become friends with his new wife. But it isn't easy. And now Abdul." Her eyes fill with tears. "How could anyone kill that sweet man?"

Olivia and I exchange glances over our friend's head. I wish we could help her, but I have no idea what to do.

"Vivian, Kadem's new wife, is British and quite reserved. She likes to run the house like a military base, and you know me, Julia. An orderly existence has never been my thing. We came here because Peter's father insisted he couldn't run his business without his son, but now…well, I don't know." She pauses. "I miss home."

I can understand this. Mal was born in Morocco but moved with her family to the States when she was one year old. She met Peter when they were both in graduate school.

She twists a tissue in her hands. "I wish Vivian would quit telling me what I have to do to be socially acceptable. I'm not changing the way I behave. And she's in such a tizzy about our party. Am I sure I have the correct food ordered? Have I told the staff exactly what to do? She's making me crazy."

Lordy! Now she's making me crazy, and I don't even know the lady. I can only imagine what her reaction will be to key lime pie. But at the moment, I'm not thinking about pie. I'm thinking about the poor dead man on the driveway. I'd like to ask if anyone is attending to him, but I don't want to upset Mal more than she is.

"I wish we didn't have to live in this house." Mal makes a sweeping motion with her hand, nearly knocking over a cloisonné vase. "It's too big, and there are people everywhere. I feel like someone is watching everything I do. I told Peter if we had to live in this city, at least I wanted our own place, but he said that would hurt his father's feelings."

I had to agree with her about the house being big. When I saw first saw it, I thought it had to be a hotel because it's way too grandiose to be a home. It's built in a U-shape, and it's enormous. There's a dome on the roof and red rosebushes line both sides of a long drive, and elaborate mosaics frame the front door.

"Vivian is very efficient," Mal continues. "I feel a bit sorry for Kadem because Fatima, Peter's mother, was lovely. Both he and Peter were devastated when she died of cancer. Slowly, Vivian is removing all traces of her in this house. I don't know," she says doubtfully, "maybe Kadem likes all the organization. Vivian went through boxes of stuff that belonged to Fatima and threw out most of it. Even searched her jewelry, and that's when the real trouble started. A very precious, expensive ruby ring is missing. Vivian came down the stairs screeching like a banshee that the Kettani Ruby was gone." A slight grin plays around Mal's lips. "It was the first time I ever saw her hair disheveled. It usually looks like it's cemented in place."

"What do you think happened to the ring?"

She shrugs. "I have no idea. Neither does Peter or his father. No one can remember the last time anyone saw it because it was far too valuable to wear."

This is fascinating. "How did Vivian know about it?"

"Lots of people in Marrakech know about the Kettani Ruby. Can you imagine? Both words are capitalized because it's so well-known and fabulous. Sort of like the Holy Grail. Kadem's father bought it in Burma—or Myanmar—many years ago. The ruby is set in platinum, surrounded by small diamonds. I think the value is around $17,000,000. It should have been in a vault in the bank, but there's a sophisticated, impenetrable safe in this house. The ring was in there, along with other valuable jewelry. When Vivian couldn't find it, she had the staff turn the house upside down looking for it."

I know my jaw is hanging open, and I struggle to close it. "How could it disappear from the safe?"

"That's a great question. No one knows. Someone had to take it out of the safe and only Peter's father and his deceased wife knew the combination."

This is, indeed, a mystery. "So the present Madam Kettani doesn't know how to open the safe?" I ask.

Mal shakes her head. "No. She told Kadem she had some jewelry she wanted to put away for safe keeping, and that's when they discovered the ring was missing. I have to tell you, Julia, this whole thing has made living here very unpleasant. There's so much gossip and finger pointing. Vivian tried to blame the staff, but that was a ridiculous idea. And now on top of this, poor Abdul is dead. It's terrible." She abruptly changes the subject. "I'm so excited about having you and Olivia here. And I drool thinking about the key lime pie."

Olivia, who'd been listening until now, says, "It sounds like you have a lot going on. Are you certain you still want to do this? Maybe this isn't the best time to have a party. We're happy to make the pies, but…are you sure?"

"Positive. There's no way we can cancel now. Invitations were sent out a long time ago. Don't worry." She squares her shoulders. "The pie will be the perfect ending to our dinner." When she sees the skepticism on our faces, she says, "I promise. Now let's go find the others. Peter and his dad will be there. Vivian, too. I can't wait for you to meet her."

I can wait. Vivian sounds like a barracuda.

Peter and his new step-mother are waiting for us in what Mal calls the "cozy nook." It's a lovely room filled with turquoise and raspberry comfortable couches, red and green Berber rugs, sheer turquoise curtains at the floor to ceiling windows, and flowers everywhere. My entire house in Wake Forest would fit into one end of it.

Peter is handsome as ever. He's very tall, has thick black hair, dark eyes, and bronze skin. When he stands next to Mal——who is also tall, has sleek black hair, lively eyes and a fit, athletic body——they make an awesome couple.

The new Mme. Kettani is probably in her mid-fifties, but thanks to what I suspect is a vigorous regime of Botox, fillers and laser treatments, looks younger. She is almost too slim and wears her dark hair swept back into an elaborate twist. She's dressed in a long, deep purple flowing gown with a red sash.

She sweeps over to me and extends a hand. "I understand you'll be helping with the cooking. I'm sure you'll find our kitchen adequate."

Mal's eyes narrow. "She's not helping with the cooking, Vivian. I've told you this before. She's a guest, and she and Olivia are going to make their fabulous dessert. It will be a wonderful ending to our meal." She puts her arm around my waist. "Julia and Olivia are my very good friends."

But Vivian isn't listening. She's stopped a maid carrying a platter of smoked salmon and is eyeing it critically. "Please take this back and tell cook I don't want capers on the tray. I believe I've told her this before."

I hear voices in the hall, and Kadem enters the room, a frown on his face. When he sees us, he smiles and greets us warmly. Olivia and I met him when he and Peter's mother came to Chapel

Hill to visit their son. Now he seems genuinely happy to see us. Shorter than his new wife, he has grey hair and an impressive moustache.

"Sorry about that unpleasant business outside. The police think Abdul was robbed. When he tried to resist, he was killed." The frown on his face deepens. "Please forgive me, but I must leave now. I must go to his family."

We mumble our goodbyes and then stand around awkwardly, trying not to listen to Vivian's voice as she gives orders. When she finishes with the maid, she turns her attention to Peter.

"Nabil, could you please instruct your driver to garage your car when you're not using it. It looks unsightly sitting out."

Peter flinches visibly. "I've asked you many times to call me Peter, Vivian. I haven't used my Moroccan name for years."

She pats his arm. "You're home now. You're not in America anymore. Here your name is Nabil."

Mal pulls me away. "I'm sorry about this. What Vivian said to you is hateful. She knows perfectly well you and Olivia are my good friends."

"Don't worry about it." The truth is, I'm suddenly so tired Vivian could have accused me of stealing the Kettani Ruby, and I wouldn't have cared. "Olivia and I need to go to bed," I tell her. "We can chat tomorrow."

As we walk through the house, I see movement out of the corner of my eye. An older woman wearing an apron over a djellaba peers at us from an open crack in a door. When she sees me looking at her, she crooks her finger and motions for me to come to her. But I can't do that because Mal is walking briskly to the front door, and she's holding my arm. Suddenly I feel our good friend is trying to get rid of us.

"Until tomorrow," Mal says as we reach her car. "Sleep well."

"Right. Take it easy, Mal." I want to say more, but Mal has already turned around and is practically sprinting into the house.

Chapter 2

Aziz, Mal's driver, opens the door to a snazzy black Mercedes and waits for us to climb in. I've made reservations at a small hotel in the city, so I try to hand him a paper with the name of the place, but he waves my hand away.

"That's not necessary, madam. Madam Kettani has given me instructions."

"That can't be," I say to Olivia. "I didn't tell Mal where we were staying."

"Maybe he doesn't understand you," Olivia says. "Try again."

"I've booked a room at this place," I say, trying once more to hand him the paper. "Could we please go there?"

But Aziz isn't listening. *Maybe I did tell Mal the name of the hotel. Did I?* I guess I'm too tired to remember. I give up trying to think and settle back in the seat as the Mercedes purrs to life and silently rolls away.

Olivia and I don't talk much in the car. As we drive through the unfamiliar streets I feel my eyes fall shut. When I open them briefly, I see Olivia is snoozing, too. Jet lag has set in. I honestly didn't think I was sleeping, but when a voice says, "We are here, madam," I jerk upright and realize I've been dreaming and am not baking cupcakes in an airplane galley with Buddy Valastro, the Cake Boss.

I look out the window and think Aziz has made a mistake.

When the car sighs to a stop in front of a building with a magnificent front door and I see two elegantly dressed doormen, I'm sure he's made a mistake. This definitely does not look like the modest hotel I found online. I tap Aziz on the shoulder. "Excuse me, but I think this is wrong. This isn't our hotel."

"Indeed, it is, madam. I have explicit orders. Madam Kettani said to bring you here. She will call you later to see if you are comfortable. Please go inside. I'll attend to the luggage."

Before we took this trip, I read a lot about Marrakech because I like to know where I'm going. So I know that Olivia and I are standing in front of the famous and fabulous La Mamounia hotel —a luxurious oasis for glittery people—and it costs a boatload of money to stay here. Olivia and I are neither glittery nor in possession of boatloads of money. And we sure aren't dressed for the venue.

Aziz gives us a reassuring smile. "They are expecting you, madam. Your room is ready."

Olivia's eyes are as big as saucers. "Did you reserve a room here, Julia? This is quite awesome."

"I certainly didn't. Aziz must have made a mistake, and I'll clear it up." In a minute. But first I have to gawk at the magnificent front door, which two smiling doormen, each dressed in full length maroon velvet capes, white gloves and white caps on their heads hold open for us.

"There's no point in arguing," I say. Let's go in and see what's going on. I'll bet once they see us, they'll figure out they've made a mistake."

I'm not being mean. We just don't look like Mamounia material. We've been traveling for thirty-six hours and are wearing jeans, T-shirts and tennis shoes. The elegant lady who just passed us on the steps looks right at home in a camel-colored straight skirt, black jacket over crisp white shirt and black patent leather heels. We don't.

Olivia tries to hide a coffee stain on her shirt. "We really look out of place."

I link my arm in hers. "Come on. We'll find out it's a mistake and that will be that."

But it isn't a mistake. We're met at the door by Salma, a smiling woman who speaks flawless English and invites us to sit down on a leather couch while she offers us almond milk and dates and tells us about our accommodations.

I'm trying to listen to her, but Olivia and I are speechless. The lobby is enormous, and there's a magnificent crystal chandelier hanging over a gigantic statue in the middle of the marble floor. And flowers everywhere! Vases of fragrant pink roses and lilies and orange blossoms. And vibrant mosaic tiles. I feel like I'm a character in a Moorish fairytale.

Olivia starts to laugh. "I'm thinking about the last time I checked into a motel. There was a half empty paper cup of coffee with a cigarette butt floating in it on the counter. This sure is different"

It sure is different, and I'm still convinced this has to be a big mistake. I protest again and try to assure Salma that neither Olivia nor I can afford this obvious luxury, but she laughs and asks us to follow her. An elevator purrs to the top floor, and she throws open a door to reveal about the most astonishing rooms I've ever seen.

There's a bedroom for each of us and marble everywhere and graceful arches and wooden beams and intricate mosaics and an exquisite ceiling crafted with inlaid mahogany. The bathroom has more marble and a huge porcelain tub with claw feet and gold fixtures. A gold blanket is folded over crisp white linens on a huge bed. Red velvet chairs, a writing desk and more wonderful colorful mosaic tiles. And tapestries. Oh my, the tapestries!

Salma opens heavy taffeta and silk drapes to reveal a balcony with comfortable furniture and a glorious garden with the snowcapped Atlas mountains in the background. She smiles. "Madam Kettani said you would enjoy this view."

The view leaves me speechless. I see olive trees and blooming jasmine, and smell the fragrant aroma of orange and lemon blossoms and rows of roses. It's spectacular and convinces me more than ever that someone has made a dreadful mistake. I try to tell this to Salma, but she waves my words away.

"Please enjoy your evening. And perhaps a bit of dinner on your balcony? Let us know what we can do to make your stay more comfortable."

I want to protest again, but Salma has backed out the door and closed it silently.

"This is amazing," Olivia says, "and it's no mistake." She takes a sip of an excellent white wine and settles against the cushions on her chair. She's wearing a flowing lemon-yellow caftan and has twisted her hair into a pile on top of her head. As usual, she looks great.

"Nope, it's no mistake. It's wonderful of Mal to do this." I've showered, am now dressed in comfortable pajamas and am sitting with Olivia on our balcony enjoying the wine and a platter of delicious grilled shrimp. The setting sun has turned the garden below a soft golden color, and the air is heavy with the intoxicating scent of blooming flowers.

I found the note from Mal just as Olivia and I were ready to sneak out before anyone could charge us for the dates and almond milk.

My dear friends, Julia and Olivia,

Peter and I want you to enjoy your stay here. I know what you're worrying about, Julia, so please know the bill has been taken care of. All you have to do is relax and eat. We are so happy you're here. All my love, Mal.

What a wonderful friend! Mal had invited us to stay in the Kettani home, but Olivia and I decided we wanted to stay in a hotel. That way we'd be free to do a bit of sightseeing and exploring the city. I'd booked a reasonably priced room at a little hotel in the heart of Marrakech. Staying at the luxurious La Mamounia never entered our minds. But here we are. And it's fabulous.

"I can't wait to see Oliver's reaction when he hears where we're staying," Olivia says.

"Oliver travels a lot. Maybe he's been here," I say.

After three bad marriages, Olivia had sworn off men for good —until last year when she met Oliver Parker-Smythe. Oliver lives in England, has a boat and a plane and a bunch of sheep and is just about the nicest guy you'll ever meet. There was instant chemistry between the two. At the end of this week, he's picking up Dirk Harrison and the two are flying to Marrakech. Dirk is a lawyer in Sacramento and is coming to see me. I, too, had sworn off men because I had a really good husband until he was killed, and after that I figured there was no one in the world who could live up to the one I'd lost so why bother—until I met Dirk.

Now I guess you can say both Olivia and I are smitten. I can also say I've never seen Olivia happier, and that's saying a lot because we grew up together in South Carolina, so I've seen all the ups and downs in her life.

"I have to admit I'm looking forward to seeing him," she says, and I laugh when a scarlet flush spreads over her face. She changes the subject quickly. "So what do you make of the whole missing ring thing?" She piles shrimp on her plate and selects a hunk of bread. "Could you pass me that bowl of fruit, too? The mango looks sensational."

"I don't know, but I have a feeling in my gut something's wrong. Mal looks tired. Did you notice she has circles under her eyes? Maybe it's just the stress of adjusting to new surroundings. It can't be easy living in that house. And was she trying to get us to leave or was I imagining that."

"I couldn't live twenty minutes with that new missus," Olivia says. "I'm sure she's a lovely lady, but she's a bit too bossy for me."

I nod. "I felt sorry for Peter. His mother was such a wonderful person. Genuinely warm and nice. She knew his American name was Peter and never objected."

Olivia stands up to pour more wine in our glasses. "It's not up to this new person to object. I mean, even we know Peter better than this woman does."

"We do, indeed." My phone pings, and I see there's a message from Mal. *So sorry about today. Hope you and Olivia are enjoying yourselves there. I've arranged for Aziz to take you on a little shopping trip tomorrow morning. See you after that. Sweet dreams, Mal.*

I read the message to Olivia and say, "I'd like to find something to take back home and put on a shelf in Little Bites, so when we're working our tails off, we can look at it and remember all this luxury."

"Mmm. Okay." She points to an item on the room service menu. "We haven't had a proper meal today. Do you think it would be possible to order an omelet? I'm really hungry."

"Only one way to find out," I say, picking up the phone. "I think I'll have one, too. And maybe a small filet? And these potatoes sound delicious. How about you?"

"Sounds perfect." Olivia smiles happily. "Maybe a bit more wine, too. After all, we have to have something to wash it all down."

An hour later, we are both almost comatose from too much food. As I waddle off to bed, I say, "The day had a bit of a rough beginning, but the ending is quite satisfactory." And so is the bed. I'm asleep before I remember to text Millie, my dog sitter, to ask how my puppies are doing.

Chapter 3

Crossing a busy street in Marrakech reminds me of the time Polly Presley dared me to jump off Johnson's garage roof into a pile of leaves. I closed my eyes, held my breath and went for it. Not the smartest thing I've ever done, and I ended up with a broken arm. I'm doing the same thing today, and I'm hoping it doesn't result in the same ending. Aziz is holding both Olivia and me firmly by our elbows and urging us to move. My eyes are closed, but I can hear cars whizzing by, horns honking and the occasional screeching of brakes. When I do open them briefly, I see crosswalks and traffic lights have little significance. Cars zip through red, stop on green and make U-turns in the middle of the street. Aziz puts his hand out to halt a speeding vehicle, hauls us across on red and deposits us safely on the other side.

"We are going to visit the most famous square in all of Marrakech," Aziz says. "I know you will enjoy it. You can buy many things."

I want to tell this nice man that dodging traffic has rattled my nerves, and Olivia and I are still exhausted from the trip and probably would rather still be in bed, but he is so enthusiastic I don't have the heart to disappoint him.

The scene at Jemaa el Fna is unlike anything I've ever seen. The huge square in the Old City throbs with hundreds of people. At first glance it resembles a spectacular circus with lots of different acts performing at once.

An acrobat team made up of young men dressed in shiny green pants and shirts creates a human pyramid. A man with a leathery face and missing teeth wraps a cobra around his neck. He holds the snake's head in his hand and laughs when I back away.

There is a dentist pulling teeth. I don't want to watch, but it's like a train wreck. I can't look away. The unlucky patient sits in a chair, and the dentist uses a pair of pliers for the extraction.

I'm mesmerized by the sight of a man wearing the traditional red Rifi costume and a wide-brimmed straw hat with tassels. He approaches us and offers me a drink of water from a ladle. "He's selling water. He wants you to give him money," Aziz says.

"Please tell him no thank you. I think I can see the amoebae swarming on that ladle from here."

Olivia points to a group of people gathered around a man sitting on a stool. They're laughing and clapping and obviously having a good time. "What are they doing? It must be fun."

"They're listening to a story teller," Aziz says. "He comes every day to tell different stories, and people love listening."

"It's too bad we can't understand him," I reply. "From the way the crowd is laughing, it must be quite good."

Aziz hurries us through the throng of people and into the souks at the end of the square. We enter a dizzying complex of open shops and twisting alleyways, and it's so crowded it's hard to walk without banging into someone, but no one seems to mind. This is shopping like I've never seen before. There are stalls everywhere—each one tended by a smiling merchant who shouts at us to come in and have tea. Eager boys run after us, offering to be our guides until they spot Aziz and melt into the crowd. The hot air is thick with cigarette smoke and unfamiliar smells. I take Olivia by the arm and say, "We should probably stay attached to each other. I'd hate to get lost in here."

Such a cacophony of sounds and colors and smells! At one stall I marvel at the dripping skeins of bright red, blue and yellow dyed wool hanging up to dry. Another stall has mounds of aromatic spices— brilliant yellow saffron, red paprika and orange turmeric. And fabrics—bolts of the most gorgeous cloth. And copper pots. And shoes. At one shop a man sits on the ground sewing slippers, and the smell of leather is overpowering.

Aziz leads us to a stall and says, "Look here. There are nice things." He points to a table full of jewelry that is almost too shiny to be real. There are bright red and purple stones, deep green teardrops and pure white stones with streaks of purple hanging from chains or made into rings and pins. "These are all handmade, and you can buy here. He will not cheat you."

I hadn't planned to do any jewelry shopping, but I'd like to have something from Marrakech to take home. "What do you think?" I ask Olivia. "Shall we buy something?"

My friend is already holding a string of green beads and listening to the merchant tell her they are onyx from the Atlas mountains. She puts them up to her neck and looks into a small mirror. "They may not be real, but they're pretty. I think I'll get them."

I'm eyeing a necklace with a significant green oval stone on a gold chain. The stone is surrounded by tiny purple stones.

The piece has a bit of heft to it, which makes me hope it won't turn green on my neck right away. The merchant slides over to me and smiles broadly. "I have others that would be better with your eyes."

"That's okay," I tell him. "I like this one very much."

He frowns and tries to take it out of my hand. "This one not so good. I have better."

"That's okay," I say again, giving the necklace a tug. "I want this one."

He shows me a necklace with a gaudy red stone mounted in a gold setting. "Look here, madam. Real diamonds" He uses a grimy finger to point out the glittery stones in the setting. "I give you good price."

I shake my head and hold the necklace with the green stone securely in my hand. "How much?"

The shop keeper folds his arms across his chest and glares at me.

Aziz steps up and says something that makes the merchant's face turn purple. There's a lot of handwaving and loud words and finally Aziz turns to me. "He says the price is 500 dirham. I told him that is too expensive. Shall we go?"

I mentally convert dirham to dollars. $47 does seem like a lot for a hunk of what is probably glass, but now I absolutely have to have this. I turn to Aziz. "How much is the one he wants me to buy?"

"1000 dirham."

"Well, then. This is a deal." I hand the shop keeper the money and without waiting for a bag, stick the necklace in my purse. As we walk away I feel the merchant's eyes boring into my back.

"I am so sorry, madam. You paid him too much." Aziz says. "That man was not the usual shopkeeper. My friend would not have cheated you."

He looks so distressed I have to resist the urge to hug him and tell him it's okay. I smile and say, "Please don't worry. I really like this little necklace, and it will always remind me of this wonderful trip."

He brightens instantly and guides us out of the souks. "Madam Kettani has instructed me to bring you to her house in two hours. Will that be enough time for you to rest? She's anxious to see the dessert you prepare."

Olivia and I exchange glances. We crawled out of bed to meet Aziz early this morning so we both need to shower, unpack our clothes, wash our hair and maybe take a nap. Two hours doesn't sound like enough time. However, we didn't come to Morocco to sleep.

"That sounds wonderful. We'll be ready," I tell him. "There's one more thing we'd like to do before we go back to the hotel. Can you please take us somewhere to buy wine? I feel we're going to need it."

Aziz smiles. "Let me organize that for you, madam. I know just the place, and I'll have it brought to your room."

I pull money out of my wallet and hand it to him. "That would be marvelous. Thank you. We'll be ready to go with you soon." Maybe if I skip the shower, forgo clean hair and fall right into bed as soon as we reach our room, I'll feel less like a zombie and more like Mal's old friend.

Chapter 4

The kitchen is big, hot and noisy. There are busy people everywhere—cooking, chopping and chattering. As soon as we enter, the chatter stops. Mal pulls me toward a woman bent over a large pot and holding a wooden spoon.

"This is Suad. She's our cook and in charge of this madness. I think we have everything you put on your list. She'll show you where we stored it."

Suad greets me with a smile and a torrent of words I don't understand.

"Oh my, Suad only speaks Arabic and French." Mal looks at me hopefully. "Are you possibly able to speak either?"

I shake my head. My French is limited to *Voulez vous coucher avec moi?* and I'm not going to say that.

Mal's cell phone suddenly begins to play *I Wanna Dance With Somebody* and she glances at it without answering and sticks it back in her pocket. "I've got to go. There's the stove, and there are pots and pans, and you'll find stuff in the fridge. I'm sure you'll be fine. Have fun."

She's gone before I can ask how to call for help in French. The other women, who had pulled back when Mal was in the kitchen, now move toward us.

"I think they're curious," I say to Olivia. "Just smile pleasantly."

"I think we're in over our heads," she whispers. "This is kind of daunting."

"Nonsense. We just need to figure out where everything is."

The kitchen is an eclectic mixture of Moroccan mosaic tiles, marble counters and modern appliances. I open the door of a huge Sub-Zero refrigerator and peer inside. Sure enough, one side of a shelf is labeled "Julia" and contains cans of sweetened condensed milk, butter, eggs and cartons of heavy cream. I almost panic when I don't see limes, but Olivia locates a full basket of them on the floor.

I find measuring cups and spoons, but they aren't going to help me because all the measurements are in grams so I'm going to have to eyeball the ingredients, which may or may not turn out well. I brought several boxes of graham crackers with me. Judging from their squashed appearance, I'd say the crackers aren't going to need much smashing. I'm so busy, I don't realize Suad is standing behind me until I turn around and nearly bang into her. She motions for me to follow her.

She points to the oven and smiles broadly. "Is good."

I smile too. "It smells wonderful."

She moves aside, raises her eyebrows and points to the oven door, indicating I should open it. When I hesitate, she does it for me, and I behold a gorgeous piece of beef roasting in an onion sauce. It looks amazing, and I guess my expression tells her how much I like it because she pulls me around the kitchen and shows me tagines of beef and chicken, and mountains of fresh fruit, and all kinds of fresh vegetables. The meal is going to be sensational, and I'm hoping Mal's guests will enjoy our key lime pie. Its tart, refreshing taste should make a nice ending to a meal of spicy meats.

I find a space on a counter and get to work smashing what's left of the whole graham crackers, adding melted butter and brown sugar and pressing the mixture into the aluminum foil pie pans I brought with me. When I have eight pans ready, I put them in an oven to bake for eight minutes. Every time I look up, Suad is beaming at me.

We're using real limes for this recipe—no bottled juice—and Olivia is busy cutting and squeezing them. She is also unusually silent. I pause to wipe sugar off my nose. "Something wrong?"

She shakes her head. "Just listening."

"You mean you understand what they're saying?"

"Most of it."

"Really?" I give her a suspicious look. "When did you learn French?"

"It was after my second divorce. As you may remember I was a bit out of sorts back then. I felt like I had no real skills and wanted to do something different with my life, so I took several French courses. I actually became quite good at it." She smiles. "I was going to go to France and get a job. Maybe wear a beret and live on the Left Bank."

"You will never cease to amaze me," I tell her. "What are they saying? From the laughter and significant looks, I'd guess they have some juicy gossip."

She hands me a cup full of lime juice and says, "From what I can understand, they're talking about someone having a secret affair. I think it's a woman, and they're not saying very nice things about her."

I whisk the egg yolks until they're fluffy, then add some lime zest, the sweetened condensed milk and finally the lime juice.

Now I can turn my attention back to Olivia. "Are they talking about someone here in the kitchen?"

Olivia shakes her head. "I don't think so. They're not trying to be discreet. And they sure aren't treating whoever it is kindly. I think they're saying this person is married, and her husband is attractive. They think he's too good for her."

She stops talking because Suad appears and looks over my shoulder at the bowl. "Pudding?"

"Sort of." I pick up a teaspoon, stick it in the mixture and hand it to her. "Try it."

She cautiously tastes it, grimaces and hands it back. "Citron?"

"Sort of."

Judging from her reaction I'm feeling a bit nervous. I know Moroccans love sweets, and key lime pie is sweet but has a nice tartness. Maybe they won't like the tartness. I pour the filling into the pie pans and stick them in the oven for about ten minutes.

Suad glances around the kitchen and apparently satisfied no one is watching, pulls a well-worn photo out of her pocket. When I look confused, she says, "Abdul."

I don't know what to say, but since she wouldn't understand my words, I say, "I saw him lying on the ground yesterday. So sad. He must have been your good friend."

By now two other ladies have put down their cooking utensils and drifted over. "Abdul good man," one says.

"I'm sure he was."

Another points to the photo and looks at me questioningly. "You know?"

"No, I didn't know him, but he must have been very nice."

Soon the entire kitchen staff is clustered around us, all chattering at once. It's obvious they were fond of the deceased chauffeur. They are almost imploring me to give them more information, which I regrettably can't produce.

A young woman pushes her way through the group until she's in front of me. "Lady, you help us?"

I smile at her. "I don't understand what you want me to do."

She puts her hand on my arm and looks at me earnestly. "Not good in this house. Abdul knew." She says something in Arabic and the ladies all nod their heads in agreement.

I'm about to ask what Abdul knew when they suddenly fall silently and fade back to their work stations. Mal comes through the door and walks briskly over to us.

"I see you're hard at work. Did you find everything? Suad, why is this piece of meat not in the refrigerator?" She points to a slab of beef. "I told you not to leave it out. It attracts flies."

"Yes, madam." Suad picks up the offending meat and carries it away.

"You look smashing, Mal." She's wearing black pants, a beige tunic with a diamond clip on her shoulder and black high heels. Her dark hair is pulled back and twisted into a shiny bun. She has a Chanel bag over her shoulder and a turquoise folder with a silver clip in her hand. She looks expensive and impressive. "I take it you're not housecleaning today." It's meant as a joke, but Mal doesn't look amused.

"I have to meet with some bankers today, which is never fun. I'll see you later, Julia. I'm almost late. This would have to happen on the day of the party."

I have no idea what she's talking about, but I know better than to ask. "Well, whatever you're doing, you look lovely, and your party tonight will be wonderful. The ladies here are cooking up a storm."

Mal frowns as she looks around the kitchen. "I hope so. This has to be perfect. Suad, have the fresh vegetables arrived?" She picks up two green peppers. "These look old. They won't do."

As she talks, I notice some of the ladies have bowed their

heads and are exchanging sly, sideway glances. Mal does sound a bit harsh. I want to defend my friend and tell them the madam just has party jitters, but I don't want to embarrass her in front of her staff.

Mal rubs her finger around the inside of the empty filling bowl and licks it. "Just as I remember. It's perfect, Julia." She wipes her hand on a towel and says, "I'm off now. See you later. If you need anything, please ask Suad. She is happy to help. I know there's a language barrier, but you can figure it out."

As soon as Mal is out of the kitchen, I'm hoping the ladies will tell me what they meant by "Abdul know," but the obvious chatting is over—at least to us. They are all busy and silent. I pull the pies out of the oven and put them on racks to cool.

Olivia and I wash the bowls and utensils and clean off the counter. "It feels awkward in here now," Olivia says. "How long do we have to stay here?"

"As soon as these are cool enough to put in the fridge, we can go. I agree with you about the awkwardness. Mal's appearance seems to have killed the urge to talk."

Olivia shifts her eyes to two of the ladies who are whispering together. When they see us looking, they quickly go back to work. "Something's going on. I guess you'd call it palace intrigue. This is a big house with a sizeable staff. There's bound to be gossip."

I nod. "Which I wish we could understand."

Suad is wrestling with a huge shoulder of lamb. There's sweat on her brow, and her face is screwed in concentration. I walk over to admire her work.

"How will you cook that?"

When she looks at me in bewilderment, I say, "Spices?" I pick up a sprig of rosemary. "Or thyme?"

Her face lights up as she understands. "*Ah, oui.* She shows me cumin, coriander, saffron, onion, black pepper, turmeric and paprika.

"And this?" I pick up a garlic bulb.

Her face clouds, but a slight grin plays around her lips. "*Non*. Madam no like so I do this."

She makes slits in the meat, sticks in cloves, pinches it shut, then raises her eyebrows and gives me a long look.

"Don't worry, Suad. Your secret is safe with me. Madam will never know." At least not until Madam tastes the garlic.

Suad smiles shyly. "You like tea?"

"No, thank you. We don't have time." I point to my watch. "We have to go back and get ready for the party."

We quickly stow the pies in the refrigerator and as we leave, I wave to Suad. She looks up from her lamb, nods briefly and goes back to her work.

Chapter 5

The house glitters. Lovely crystal chandeliers give a warm glow to the amazing room. At least ten red velvet chairs are arranged in small groups on a gorgeous Berber rug. In the center of the room is a low, square piece of furniture covered in crimson and gold patterned velvet with a fringe of gold and red. Massive silk drapes at the floor-to-ceiling windows are tied back low to the ground, allowing them to billow artistically. There are at least ten cloisonné vases filled with fragrant pink and white roses.

And the guests glitter, too——well-dressed women in evening gowns and flowing caftans and saris, and men in elegant tuxedos or outfits of their country. I think Olivia and I are also looking pretty spiffy. She's wearing a long black gown with a crystal belt and black sandals. Her dark hair is swept up and held with a sparkly clip. I notice she's added a lot of dark eye makeup, which makes her look mysterious and exotic.

I don't look mysterious or exotic. I'm wearing my new fun necklace and my long, midnight blue dress, which was fine when we left the hotel, but I'm so nervous about the key lime pie I'm beginning to sweat. I can feel wetness in my armpits and resist the urge to flap my elbows like I'm doing the chicken dance.

"I'll be glad when this is over," I whisper to Olivia. "I can't believe I'm saying this, but I'm not even hungry."

"Well, I am." My friend helps herself to a caviar-laden toast point offered by a passing waiter. "This tastes so good. I love Mal, but you'd think she'd have offered us lunch or something. We haven't had much to eat, and it's been a long day."

"Speak of the devil." I spot Mal across the room talking to an elegantly-dressed man and woman. She has her professional smile on her face, which I recognize from the days she lectured at UNC about African art.

She sees us, waves, smiles at the couple and makes her way over. "I'm so happy you're here. I don't know most of these people, but Peter told me they're important. Do you think this dress is okay? Peter wanted me to wear it, but it's kind of heavy."

Her long dress is stunning. It's green and gold silk, three quarter length sleeves, a V-neck and elaborate gold scroll work on the front. The lush green fabric falls open at the waist to reveal another gold layer. I can imagine it's hot and heavy to wear.

"You look like a Moroccan princess," I tell her.

"She's my Moroccan princess," a voice behind me says. "It's so good to see you again, Julia. You, too, Olivia." Peter Kettani looks every inch the successful investment banker in a smashing tux. "Mal is so glad you're visiting. I think she's been a little homesick for North Carolina."

I smile. "You're looking great, Peter. Being back in Morocco must agree with you."

"It certainly has been interesting," he says.

A man approaches him and whispers in his ear. He scowls and turns to us. "Would you please excuse me? The police have more questions about Abdul. I'd hoped this could wait until the party was over."

As he walks away, I notice the look on Mal's face. "What's wrong, Moroccan Princess? The party is very successful. You did a good job."

"I don't care about the party. And don't call me that. I don't want to be a Moroccan princess. What I'd like to do is go home with you."

I'm confused. "You mean go back to La Mamounia?"

"No, I mean go back to your house in Wake Forest and forget all this nonsense."

"Are you nuts?" Olivia blurts out. "Do you remember her house? You could put the whole thing in this room."

Mal waves away a waiter with a tray of smoked salmon. "I love that house. It's so warm and cozy."

"It is?" I'm amazed. I want to find out more about her urge to return to suburbia, but now isn't the time, and I see a woman approaching with a smile on her face. "Talk tomorrow?"

She nods and turns to greet her guest, and I move away. I have to get to the kitchen and check on the pies. For the last half hour I've been imagining the power has somehow failed, and the key lime filling is now key lime juice—a sticky mess that has run all over the refrigerator. I make my way through the guests, listening to party chatter in several different languages. A tap on the shoulder makes me turn around.

"Well, hello again."

He's short, has sandy hair, a belly that indicates a fondness for beer, and looks vaguely familiar. I don't want to be rude, but I honestly have no idea who he is.

"I'm sorry. Do we…?"

"You don't recognize me, do you?"

I smile politely. "I'm afraid I don't."

"Royal Air Maroc. Flight from JFK to Marrakech. No sleep and lots of wine?"

Good grief! It's the guy from the plane. I'd been so excited about coming to Morocco, I couldn't sleep on the flight, and he and I stayed awake all night talking and drinking too much wine. And I don't recognize him because now he's wearing a tux and shiny black patent leather shoes. On the plane he was dressed in jeans, a Red Sox sweatshirt and tennis shoes.

"Of course," I say. "Ah…I guess I never expected to see you again. Certainly not here. This is a surprise."

He sticks out his hand. "Corey Fieldstone. And I haven't forgotten your name. Julia Greene. Am I right?"

I nod. This makes me the slightest bit uncomfortable. How could he remember my name? I don't even remember most of our conversation.

"Anyway," he continues, "I had to be in Marrakech on business, and my good friend, Nabil, invited me to this party."

"How nice for you. How do you and ah… Nabil… know each other?"

"He was my best buddy at UNC when we both were studying and partying."

I mentally try to place him in our group of friends at UNC. I sure don't remember seeing him there. Mal, Peter and I were grad students. I dropped out to marry my Tony, but Mal received a master's degree in art history and Peter earned a law degree. And we were actually intent on our studies, so there wasn't a lot of partying.

"I guess I must have missed you," I say. "I went to UNC, too. That's where I met the Kettanis, except they weren't married then."

He looks startled. "You went to UNC?"

I laugh. "What did we talk about on the plane? I live in North

Carolina and have for quite a while. Malika Kettani used to visit our lunchroom. She's been my good friend for years."

"I'm amazed. On the plane you talked about your trips to Iceland and Alaska, but never mentioned anything about North Carolina. For some reason I assumed you were from New York." He pauses, "Where are you staying here?"

Now I pause. It's an innocent question, but for some reason I feel uncomfortable answering. He can find out if he asks Mal, though, so I say, "Olivia and I are at La Mamounia."

He whistles. "Wow! That costs some serious coin. You must be doing okay. What kind of sightseeing have you been doing? I'll bet that hotel can arrange some fancy tours."

I can tell the man wants to chat, but this isn't a good time. I need to wrap this conversation up.

"I've been to the famous square and the souks."

He points to my necklace. "Is that where you bought that handsome pendant?"

"It is. It's probably glass but it'll be a fun souvenir to take back home. I hope you won't think I'm being rude, but I have to get to the kitchen and check on the dessert."

He gives me an odd look, but I don't want to explain. "It's been very nice seeing you again. Enjoy the party and your stay in Marrakech."

I walk away before he can say more, and I mentally put him on my list of things to talk about with Mal tomorrow.

Chapter 6

The kitchen smells amazing, and the room is bustling with activity. Women are mixing, chopping and chattering. The lamb Suad wrestled with earlier in the day has been roasted to perfection and rests on a wooden board waiting to be sliced. I notice cloves of garlic are nowhere to be seen.

I check my key lime pies in the fridge and am relieved to see they have set nicely. When the guests begin to eat, I'll pull them out and divide them into individual portions. I had planned on topping each slice with a dollop of whipped cream, but now that seems like overkill.

I'm about to leave the kitchen when I spot Suad standing by herself in a corner. I go over, smile and say, "It all looks wonderful. You did a great job."

I know she can't understand me, but when I smile she usually smiles back. Now her face looks like it's carved in stone. "Is something wrong? I know you probably don't know what I'm saying, but…"

She takes my hand and pulls me over to a counter. She says

something to a young girl peeling oranges, and the girl quickly moves away.

"You look." She points to an array of kitchen utensils.

"What am I looking at, Suad? I don't understand."

She pulls me closer. "You look there." She inclines her head at a wooden knife block holding a variety of different size knives. "You see?" Her finger slides forward and points to a slot. "Gone."

"What? The knife is gone?"

She puts a finger to her lips and nods her head. "Abdul."

My blood suddenly turns to ice. "Are you saying what I think you're saying—that this knife had something to do with Abdul's death?"

She doesn't need to answer. The look on her face tells me all I need to know.

Good grief! "Wait here," I tell her. "Don't move. I'm going to get Olivia. Do you understand me? Please wait right here."

I don't know how—maybe she can hear the urgency in my voice—but she folds her arms across her stomach and leans against the counter. I think she intends to do as I asked. I rush out of the kitchen and make my way through the throng of people as I look for my friend. I find her deep in conversation with a woman dressed in a gorgeous blue and purple sari. I wiggle my eyebrows at Olivia until she finally sees me and makes her excuses to the woman. I'm nearly hopping around in a nervous frenzy.

"You have to come with me. How well do you think you can speak French? Be honest. This is no time to embellish," I say as I walk briskly to the kitchen.

"What on earth is wrong with you? And why are you acting like your hair is on fire? To answer your question, I'm pretty good at conversational French. Nothing fancy. I suppose food topics are my favorite. Would you please tell me why we're walking so fast?"

We reach the kitchen and I scan the room looking for Suad. Miraculously, she's standing where I left her. We skid to a stop in front of her, and I pull Olivia forward. "Ask her if she thinks the missing knife killed Abdul?"

Olivia gives me the arched eyebrow-have-you-gone-nuts look. "Want to bring me up to speed? I have no idea what you're talking about."

I try to quickly fill her in, but Suad is already talking. She has grabbed Olivia's arm and is urgently trying to tell her something. I watch in awe as my friend calmly nods her head and replies in French. When I can stand it no longer, I blurt out, "What did she say? What did you say? Why, oh why didn't I take French in school?"

Olivia pats Suad's arm and turns to me. "You were right. She said she thinks the knife that killed Abdul came from this block."

"I don't understand. How would she know that?"

"We were just getting to that." She and the cook resume talking while I twitch nervously.

When Suad reaches into the voluminous garment she's wearing and pulls out a knife, I almost stop breathing. She holds the wooden handle between thumb and forefinger and shows it to us. There is a dried brown substance on the blade. She shifts her eyes from the knife to the empty slot in the block. "C*omprenez vous*?"

"Suad!" I almost screech. "Where did you find this? We should give it to the police."

Olivia translates and Suad shakes her head violently. "*Non.*"

"But why not. This is valuable evidence."

More conversation follows, and when Suad finally stops talking, Olivia doesn't look happy. "This isn't good, Julia. In fact,

I can hardly believe it."

"Believe what? Will you please tell me what's going on."

"Suad says one of the maids found the knife—I really don't want to say this."

"Say what? Honestly, Olivia, you are really beginning to annoy me."

"Okay. Suad says one of the maids found the knife in the back garden when she went there to pick roses. Not far from Mal and Peter's quarters. It's not possible to reach this section of the garden from the street, so whoever put it there…well, you know. She brought the knife to Suad because Suad is the unofficial head of the staff. She's the oldest and has been here the longest."

"Shouldn't she have reported this to M. or Mme. Kettani?"

Olivia chews on her lower lip. "It seems relations between the family and the staff have been strained since Fatima Kettani died. The staff is having a hard time adjusting to the new wife but feels very loyal to M. Kettani. Suad said she feels an obligation to protect him. I think we were right when we said there was a lot of palace gossip." She pauses. "Apparently, there's some gossip about Peter and Mal."

"What on earth can they say about Peter and Mal? They haven't been here long enough to cause any gossip." I say this with a bit of hesitation, though, because I'm remembering Mal's last words to us. "So this means Abdul probably wasn't stabbed in the street, and it wasn't a random robbery."

"Exactly." Olivia shudders. "It looks like someone in this house killed him."

Lordy! How on earth did we get involved in this? "Tell Suad she has to give the knife to M. Kettani," I say to Olivia. "This is nuts."

Olivia relays the message, and when Suad violently shakes her head, I don't need a translator to give me her answer.

"So what do we do now?"

"Suad says she'll put the knife in a safe place." She pauses. "She doesn't trust anyone in the house and, she wants us to figure out who killed him."

"Did you tell her that would be practically impossible to do? Someone needs to go to the police."

Olivia gives me a hard look. "Do you want to do that?"

"Certainly not. It's not up to us. We're guests here, for heaven's sake."

"So do we tell Mal?"

"Maybe tomorrow. Right now I want to cut my pies and then go back to the hotel and dream about somewhere safe—like Wake Forest. Home has never looked so good."

"What do I tell Suad?" Olivia asks.

I look at her helplessly. "What on earth can we do? We don't speak the language—at least I don't—and the only people we know are Peter and Mal."

"Well, think of something. She's gripping my arm so tightly I think my hand is going numb."

I smile at Suad. "Okay. It will be okay."

She lets go of Olivia and sinks down in a chair, relief flooding her face. "Thank you," she says in halting English. "Thank you."

When I turn away from Suad, I see Mal is in the kitchen. She's at the stove checking the tajines of chicken ready to be served. Did she hear our conversation? I can't tell. She says something to one of the cooks and leaves the room without looking at us or speaking.

The next hour passes in a blur as I put slices of key lime pie on serving platters and cross my fingers as a girl carries them out of the kitchen. I'm also trying to avoid looking at Olivia because I know she thinks I'm crazy.

I fidget as I wait to see if the guests actually eat it, and when the girl comes back in the kitchen with an empty platter and demands more, I am almost jubilant. When Olivia and I finally leave the kitchen, Suad is standing at the door. She smiles and hands me a piece of paper. She pats my arm and struggles to say more, but the words won't come. I stick the paper in my purse and forget about it until the next day.

Chapter 7

"Cheers!" I say to Olivia as we clink Bloody Mary glasses. We're having a splendid breakfast by the pool at Mamounia. The scent of jasmine mingled with the aroma of coffee and bacon is just about perfect. So are the scrambled eggs, smoked salmon and delicious rolls.

I'm beyond relieved my key lime pie was well received by Mal's guests, and to tell the truth, I think secretly she also was. As we were leaving last night, she gave me a hug and said, "You're wonderful. Thank you a million times. You should have heard all the nice things people said."

So this morning I lean back in my chair, content with the world. The party was perfect, and yesterday Aziz had ten bottles of a lovely Chablis delivered to our room, so if things get too bad, we can drown ourselves in an excellent wine.

Olivia finishes her omelet and pushes her plate away. "Now that the worry about the pies is over, we can enjoy ourselves a bit. I wouldn't mind more shopping."

I hate to leave this gorgeous place, but we didn't come here to sit in a garden. When I fish in my purse for lipstick, I notice the note Suad slipped to me last night and pull it out for a look. There's an address and the printed words, YOU GO PLEASE. 8:00 TOMORROW. I push it across the table to Olivia. "What do you make of this?"

She shakes her head. "No idea. What do you suppose we'd find at this address? You don't intend to go, do you?"

"I don't know. I mean, we did say we'd try to help find Abdul's killer. This obviously has something to do with that."

Olivia frowns. "You do realize this whole idea of us helping is absurd. We're outsiders, and we have no idea what's been happening in that house. I think we should get on with our sightseeing and leave all this intrigue where it belongs—with them, not with us."

I put the note back in my purse. "I'm sure you're right. I guess I'll think about it. I keep seeing Suad's anguished face and the relief she felt when I told her it would be okay."

"You probably shouldn't have said that. This isn't our business, Julia. Leave it alone."

"Maybe I'll have a chat with Mal and tell her about the knife. I don't want to betray Suad, but someone in the family should know. And speaking of Mal, don't you think it was strange she didn't speak to us in the kitchen last night? I'm wondering if she heard our conversation. She probably wouldn't like the idea of us snooping around."

But Olivia isn't listening to me. She inclines her head to the right and says, "Look over there at those people being seated. Isn't that Vivian and aren't those the people from the party?"

I follow Olivia's head with my eyes. "Yep. That's Corey Fieldstone and his wife. I can't remember her name."

Olivia lowers her head and looks at me. "What do we do? Do we pretend we don't see them?"

"Too late. He's waving at us. We'll have to say hello."

Reluctantly, we stand up and walk over to their table. Corey jumps to his feet and pumps my hand enthusiastically. "Wasn't it a wonderful party? Belle and I were just telling Mrs. Kettani how delicious the food was. She did a sensational job choosing the menu."

Olivia opens her mouth to set the record straight, but I step on her foot, and she glares at me instead of speaking.

"Yes, it was a great party. It's nice to see you again. Enjoy your breakfast," I say, hoping for a fast getaway.

"Nonsense. Join us." He motions for two more chairs.

"Corey, we've already eaten. We have a full day planned."

"I'm not taking no for an answer. Come. Sit."

This man is beginning to get on my nerves, and I'm about to say something rude, but Vivian pats the chair next to her. "Here, dear. This is nice. We haven't really had a chance to get acquainted." She smiles across her coffee cup. "I want to know all about you because Malika speaks of you so fondly."

I am definitely not in the mood to give her a synopsis of my life, so I say, "There's not much to tell. Olivia and I live in North Carolina, which is where we met Peter and Mal. We own a little restaurant in Wake Forest."

Her nose crinkles slightly. "I can't get used to you people from America calling him Peter. We know him as Nabil."

My brain tells me I should keep my mouth shut and be polite, but my lips don't seem to have received the message. "Yes, we call him Peter. We've known him for a very long time. Probably longer than you have."

She pats my hand and laughs. "You Americans are so outspoken. Of course I haven't known him long, but I feel as if I have. His father speaks about him all the time. I'm so happy he and Malika are here."

I don't know how to reply to this, so I say, "Corey, it's such a coincidence to see you again. I don't remember seeing your wife on the plane."

"She was sleeping, which was very smart. I had a headache the next day." He turns to his wife. "Didn't I, sweetie?"

Sweetie is short, plump, has brown, shoulder length straight hair, bangs that need trimming and apparently no voice because she nods and looks uncomfortable.

Vivian interrupts us. "Could I just ask you something about your friend, Malika?" She looks at me earnestly. "I worry that she's not happy here."

All my antennae go on high alert because I don't like discussing my friends, especially with someone I don't know. I see Olivia's eyebrows rise imperceptibly, and I know she's thinking the same thing.

"I don't think you need to worry," I say. I'm sure she's happy. It takes a while to adjust to new surroundings."

Vivian finishes her coffee and motions to a server for more. "I realize that, but Malika is Moroccan, so I'm sure she'll adapt. That's not what I'm talking about." She lowers her voice and leans closer to me. "I'm just wondering if she's having…ah… financial difficulties. This is very unpleasant to say, but I found her going through a wardrobe in the former master bedroom. I could only think she was looking for money or valuables."

I feel my face flame. "First of all, Madam Kettani, Mal may have been born in Morocco, but she's an American citizen and has lived in the United States since she was one-year-old, so life here is foreign to her. And I can promise you she's not a thief. She has her own money, and I'm sure if she needed any, Peter would gladly give it to her. I have no idea why she would be looking in the wardrobe, but I'm sure she had a reason—an innocent reason."

She pulls back and says, "I'm so sorry. I truly don't mean to offend you, but I have to admit I'm worried. It would be very difficult to have any scandal associated with Nabil's wife. He's in the middle of a delicate negotiation."

"I'm sure Madam Kettani only wants what's best for her family," Corey, who has obviously been listening to our conversation, says.

I'm beginning to squirm in my chair. I absolutely do not want to discuss our good friend with either of them. "Tell me, Corey, how exactly did you meet Peter? Olivia and I knew his friends at UNC, and we don't remember you." That may sound a bit blunt, but I can't wait to hear the answer. I have to wait, though, while he selects an assortment of cheese from a platter.

"Fair enough," he says. "I didn't exactly meet him at the university. A friend of the Kettani family introduced us at a student party. But we saw each other often."

Since Peter isn't there to ask, I can't dispute what he says, but I still think it sounds sketchy. I stand up and extend my hand to Vivian.

"It's been very nice seeing you again, but Olivia and I have to go. We have a full day of sightseeing ahead of us."

Vivian holds my hand and looks at me solemnly. "I do hope we'll have a chance to chat again."

"We will. And in a few days, my good friend, Dirk Harrison, and Oliver Parker Smythe, Olivia's friend, are coming to visit. Oliver is from England, so you two should have a lot in common."

"Really? I had no idea. What part of England does he come from?"

I turn to Olivia, who says, "He lives in a village not far from London."

She frowns. “I’m afraid we won’t have much in common. I’m from the Cotswold area. I enjoyed a more rural life.”

As we walk away, Olivia says, “They’re both from the same country, for heaven’s sake. That should be enough. And I think Oliver has some land in the Cotswold. It seems to me I remember him talking about a little country home with a thatched roof and roses growing around the garden gate.” She smiles. “He said it was charming, and I would love it.”

“Well, at least we’ll have a conversation starter when we’re all together.” I check my watch. “Walk faster. You have a spa appointment and I’m supposed to meet Mal in half an hour.”

Chapter 8

Mal is trying to be normal, but I can tell something is wrong. And I can also tell she isn't listening to the jeweler describe a heavy gold bracelet.

"You won't find better quality anywhere, madam. Feel the weight. It's solid throughout."

Mal fingers it distractedly. "Yes, very nice. Do you see anything you want, Julia?"

"Are you serious? This is too rich for my blood."

I pull her aside and whisper, "Are you interested in buying something? If not, let's get out of here."

"I definitely do not want to buy anything, and I'd love to get out of here." She thanks the salesman, and we walk out of the shop into the hot sunlight. I notice a man falls into step behind us. I poke Mal in the ribs. "I don't want to alarm you, but I think a man is following us."

She laughs. "That's not a man. Don't you recognize him? That's Aziz, my driver/bodyguard. Kadem and Vivian insist I need one for my safety. Apparently, members of the Kettani family are interesting targets for kidnappers. He's a very nice man but sometimes a pain in the 'you-know-what.' I can't go anywhere without him."

"I have to admit I didn't recognize him. He looked different without his chauffeur's uniform. Is there any chance we can lose him?"

She shakes her head. "I've tried. He's very good, plus it would be impossible in all these people and traffic."

She's right about that. We're on a busy street with cars zooming around and pedestrians everywhere. As we attempt to cross, a car flies through a red light, making me jump back in fright.

"Is obeying traffic lights optional in this country?" I have to ask. "That was close."

"Crossing these streets is not for the faint of heart." Mal turns and motions to Aziz. He approaches, takes each of us by the elbow and leads us through the traffic. Miraculously, we reach the other side unscathed and in possession of all our limbs. Since I'm familiar with his street-crossing skills, I'm not surprised.

Mal stops suddenly. "I don't know about you, but I'm not in the mood to shop. How about we go back to the hotel, have coffee and talk. I've missed you so much."

"That sure does work for me."

"Great! Let me just run into this market and buy some headache medicine. Want to come with?"

I look at the extremely crowded, small store and shake my head. "Nope. I'll wait out here with Aziz."

Mal enters the shop, and Aziz looks at me shyly. "Is madam having a good trip?"

"Yes, indeed. Madam sure is." I pause before speaking again because I want to ask him something but am not sure I should. Finally, throwing caution to the wind I say, "Aziz, can you tell me something. Malika—Mme. Kettani—is my very good friend. Is she…ah…okay here? Do people like her? I ask you because you're with her a lot, and I'm worried about her."

Aziz looks at the ground, the sky, the people around him and then at me. "It's not so good here. She's not good here."

"What does that mean, Aziz? Please, tell me." I realize what I'm asking is highly inappropriate, and he could probably be fired for speaking frankly to me, but I have to know.

"Mme. Kettani is a good person, but…" He shakes his head. "She needs to leave. There is danger."

I'm about to tear my hair out from frustration. "What can possibly be the danger?"

He only has time to say, "You watch out for her," before Mal comes out of the shop and says, "Let's go. I can't wait to sit down."

We sit at a table in the magnificent garden of the Mamounia and order coffee and rolls. I'm not hungry, but I can always manage a hot, fragrant piece of pastry. Mal stirs sugar into her cup and adds milk. "This reminds me of sitting at Little Bites and eating your great cooking.'

"You have to be kidding. Look around. Does this place look like Wake Forest? And I can't bake pastries like this."

"Yours are better." I'm astounded to see a tear roll down her face. "Sorry. I guess I'm tired after the stress of organizing the party. Sometimes I do wish I was back home with you guys though."

"Aren't you happy, Mal? You have a pretty good situation here. The family home is fabulous."

She nods. "It is, but it's very confining. I'm used to earning my own money and being active. Here I'm not allowed to work and am expected to spend my days doing silly things, like nonstop shopping. You know me, Julia. I hate that." She uses the napkin to wipe her eyes. "I'm sorry if I sound scattered. I'm still so upset about Abdul. He was such a nice man. Kind, great sense of humor. How could someone kill him?"

I wish I could comfort my friend because she's genuinely upset. "What do the police say? Surely it's being investigated."

She shrugs. "Everything has been hushed up—as if it never happened. I asked Kadem, and all he said was I shouldn't worry about it. It was being taken care of. I asked him what that meant, but he didn't seem to want to explain. I know the police are treating it as a robbery because he was stabbed in the street. What I can't figure out is—if he could stagger to our driveway, why didn't he use his cell phone and call for help?"

Oh my! Here is a major dilemma. Should I tell her about the knife and where it was found? She should know this. But in the back of my mind I hear the fear in Suad's voice, and I remember the reaction when Mal walked into the kitchen.

"There's so much intrigue in the house," Mal continues, "and so much gossip." A slight tic begins to twitch under her eye, and she tries to cover it with her hand. "I do wish I could go back to Wake Forest with you. Sometimes I close my eyes and see myself sitting on your porch and chatting and laughing with you and Olivia."

I put my hand over hers. "I'm so sorry, Mal. Why don't you come back to North Carolina for a visit? I'd love to have you stay with me."

She laughs ruefully. "Can't do that, Julia. Want to know why? I don't have enough money for a plane ticket. I'd have to ask Peter to pay for it, and he wouldn't understand why I want to leave." She lifts her chin and straightens her back. "Hopefully things will change soon."

Oh my. My heart aches for Mal, but I'm also distressed

because she's treating us to our stay at La Mamounia, and considering her present situation, she shouldn't be doing that.

My friend looks at my expression and says, "I know what you're thinking, and don't worry about the hotel. Kadem is paying for that. He insisted our friends had to have first class accommodations."

Olivia and I would be perfectly happy staying in the little hotel I'd previously booked, but it's a relief to know we won't have to wash dishes to pay the bill at this one.

Her face brightens a bit. "I've been meaning to tell you—Kadem has arranged for you and Olivia to visit the Sahara Desert tomorrow—sort of a thank you for the lovely key lime pie. He has a little camp there and invites special guests to go. It's quite an experience. You can ride on a camel, sleep in a tent and have a wonderful adventure."

"That sounds marvelous. I'm sure it will be lots of fun." I pause, then say, "I'm not trying to pry, but you've always had your own money. What happened?"

She stares into her coffee cup. "We had a lot of moving expenses, and the plane tickets weren't cheap. And I had to buy fancy new clothes. We didn't have that much money when we lived in Chapel Hill, but there we didn't need it. Jeans and T-shirts were fine. Here…well, you've seen."

Indeed, I have. Vivian's friends dress as if they're having tea with the Queen.

"And I feel Vivian sort of resents me because Fatima and I were such good friends. She came to Chapel Hill to visit Peter quite often, and she and I always had a girl's day away from the men. She loved to laugh and do silly things. We became quite close."

I didn't know this. "I can understand how hard it must be for you to see Vivian running the house now," I say.

Mal looks like she's going to cry again. "You don't know the half of it. I really wish I could tell…"

"I'm sorry, madam, but we must go now." Aziz, looking uncomfortable, stands in front of us. "You're requested at home."

Mal sighs and gets to her feet. "Duty calls. I forgot Peter has invited clients for dinner. Sorry about this," she says as she gives me a hug. "It never ends."

I watch her walk away and wish I could do something to help her. I also wish she'd finished what she was trying to tell me.

Chapter 9

"Are we really going to do this?" Olivia pulls her hoodie tighter around her face and looks out the taxi window. "It's pouring out there."

Rain is pounding on the roof of the cab and flashes of lightening streak across the night sky. The driver twists around to open my door, but I'm reluctant to get out. "Up there," he says, pointing to the three-story building in front of us. Once we're safely deposited on the street, he wastes no time speeding away, sending sprays of water around our feet.

Olivia tugs at my arm. "Let's do something other than stand here. This is scary."

I look at the house and think it's scary, too. There are no lights coming from any window—no sign that anything living lives there. But this is the address on the paper Suad gave me. I tentatively pull the heavy front door open and peer inside. After allowing my eyes to adjust to the darkness, I see narrow, steep stairs leading up to a dim light.

"Good grief," Olivia whispers. "Are we going to be murdered?"

"I hope not," I whisper back. "We're Americans. I'm pretty sure we're safe. And Suad gave me this address. She wouldn't send us somewhere dangerous."

The stairs creak with each step as we slowly climb them. At the top, we see a figure emerge in a doorway.

"We should have brought a weapon," Olivia whispers. "The only thing I have is hairspray in my purse. What do you have?"

I consider the contents of my bag. I have my wallet, my passport, my phone, dog biscuits in a plastic baggie that I meant to give Bubba and Boodles, a lipstick, moisturizer I bought at JFK, a half-eaten power bar I keep forgetting to throw away, old grocery lists and a small book titled *Learn Arabic Fast*. Nothing that would slow down a potential attacker.

We reach the top, and the man, who's wearing a white robe that looks dirty in the dim light, moves aside and motions for us to enter. Next to me I hear Olivia suck in her breath. I put a smile on my face and attempt to greet him, but as soon as we're in the room, he disappears through a plastic curtain. There's a small wooden table and two chairs and a weak lightbulb hanging from a chain in the ceiling.

"I'd love to get out of here," Olivia says. "He's probably looking for his hatchet. I think we should split."

"This will be fine." I speak the words, but even I don't totally believe them. It's definitely spooky.

The man returns carrying a tray with two glasses of tea. Even in this light I can see the glasses are smudged and dirty. He puts the tray on the table and looks at us expectantly.

Olivia raises her eyebrows and mouths, "Do we have to?"

I nod. Unfortunately, we do. It would be considered extremely impolite to refuse. Even if we're in the presence of possible murderers, civility must be maintained. I pick up the glass and take a sip of the sweet lukewarm liquid and wonder how long it will take the parasites to set up a colony in my gut.

Another man in a white tunic joins us, points to the first man and says in good English, "This person in front of you is a shaman. He has great wisdom and will tell you many things. Afterward, a donation is greatly appreciated."

Beside me I feel Olivia relax. "I can't believe this. Suad has sent us to a fortune teller," she says softly.

I don't know the shaman's name, but in my mind I'm calling him Leonard. Don't ask me why. I don't even know anyone with that name. This man just reminds me of a Leonard. Anyway Leonard—through his interpreter—tells us to put out our hands into which he places beans. We are instructed to hold them for two minutes and then place them on the table.

"If they begin to move, the shaman will be able to tell you important things. If not, you may leave."

Since neither Olivia nor I recently fell off a turnip truck, we know these are Mexican jumping beans, and they jump because the worm larvae inside move when the beans are slightly warm. When she and I were growing up in South Carolina, a particularly annoying boy in the neighborhood kept some in his pocket and tried to get girls to feel them. Yuck. That still makes me shudder.

The beans on the table begin to move and Olivia and I try to look astonished. Leonard scoops them up and deposits them somewhere within the folds of his tunic.

The interpreter turns to Olivia and says, "Very good. We can begin. The great shaman says you have had great disappointment in your life, but that is changing now. You will soon be happy."

I wonder how he knows she's had great disappointment. For a while she did have a streak of bad luck. Three unsuitable husbands and three divorces. But now she's met Oliver and the two seem perfect for each other.

Now the interpreter talks to me. "You are descended from royalty. It is very exciting to see."

I begin to laugh. "I assure you, I'm not. My father is a fisherman, and my mother is a housewife."

But he's not to be deterred. "Not this generation. Many generations ago."

"Why do you get to be descended from royalty?" Olivia asks. "That doesn't seem fair. We grew up next door to each other."

"He said many generations ago. I suppose that's possible."

"Well, it's not," Olivia says. "I knew your grandparents. This whole thing is dumb."

"You have great wisdom. You have done good things," Leonard intones through the interpreter.

"So has Olivia," I say quickly because I can see thunderclouds forming in my friend's eyes.

He nods. "You are able to see inside of people. People may not be who they seem to be."

Olivia and I look at each other. "Excuse me? Could you be more specific?"

He paces around the room, his white robe swishing as he walks.

"There is untruth everywhere," the interpreter intones. "Soon it will be too late." Leonard says more, but he's mumbling, and we can't hear his words.

Suddenly he whirls around, and in perfect English says, "There is an evil one in your midst. You can find the evil one because you are one."

I have to admit he's beginning to scare me. "I can assure you, sir, I'm not evil and neither is my friend. We should be going now."

Leonard says something to the interpreter, who frowns and leaves the room.

"I totally agree. Let's go, Julia." Olivia stands up and prepares to leave, but Leonard motions to her to sit. He turns to her and begins to speak rapidly in French. This is beyond annoying because I can't understand a word, and it seems to take forever for Olivia to translate.

"He says he has to talk fast before the other guy comes back. Suad told him I understand French, and he should trust us. He says he is Abdul's brother. Shortly before he was killed Abdul gave him something to keep in case something happened to him. He wants to give it to us."

Good grief! "Why? What are we supposed to do with it?"

Olivia tries to ask him, but Leonard reaches into a pocket in his voluminous robe, pulls out a small plastic baggie and thrusts it into her hand. She barely has time to stick it in her purse before the interpreter returns holding a jar.

"We are finished now. You have your message. You can go."

He holds out the jar and shakes it. I stick 5 dirham in the slot, and Olivia and I stand up. I glance at Leonard, who has bowed his head and appears to be sleeping.

"Is he okay?" I ask the interpreter.

"He is resting. It is very tiring to reveal messages. If you would like to hear more, I will wake him."

"That won't be necessary." Olivia and I hightail it down the stairs and don't speak until we reach the street. The rain has stopped, but there are puddles on the ground, and the air smells wet.

Olivia wraps her arms around her body. "That place gave me the creeps. What on earth are we going to do now?"

"Beats me. I need to think, and for that I'm going to need a bit of wine. Let's go back to our hotel, sit on the balcony and figure this out."

The moon is full, and the intoxicating scent of citrus and date trees hangs in the air. Olivia and I are sitting on our balcony enjoying a satisfying glass of Chablis while trying to untangle recent events.

"This is what I think," I begin. "There are two forces at work here. Mal, Peter and the rest of the family are putting all their energies into a business deal. The missing ruby ring is the elephant in the room that no one wants to talk about. The family doesn't seem overly concerned about Abdul's death and consider it a robbery gone bad. The staff, on the other hand, is putting all its energies into discovering Abdul's killer. They know about the knife that killed him and know it probably came from the house, but they don't say anything because they're loyal to a fault to Kadem. And there's tension between occupants of the house—Mal included—and the staff, probably because Vivian has not so subtly suggested a staff member might be responsible for the theft of the ruby. They are also convinced the killer is someone in the house, which certainly makes them afraid to talk to anyone in the family."

I take a sip of wine and continue. "That's where we come in. Suad and the others won't go to Kadem, but they need help. We worked in the kitchen with them, so we aren't exactly fancy people. We seem to have a foot in both worlds. The question is—what do we do?"

"I don't know what we can do, Julia." In the dark I see her shake her head. "Honestly, how did we get embroiled in this?"

"I wish I could tell you. We're a long way from making key lime pies."

Olivia pulls out the baggie Leonard gave her and puts it on the table between us. "I'm almost afraid to open it. What if he's put some kind of voodoo charm in there."

"We're not in voodoo country," I tell her, picking up the baggie. "It feels like there's nothing in here." I rip it open, and a slender cylinder of metal about two inches long falls onto the palm of my hand. I hold it up so Olivia can see. "What do you suppose this is?"

"I have no idea. It looks like it might be hollow, and there's an opening on one end."

"Very odd, but it must mean something. Do you remember anything else Leonard said?"

"Nope. He kept saying 'Abdul' over and over. That man certainly was well-liked. I'm guessing this little piece of metal has to be connected to him."

The wine bottle is empty, and I consider getting another, but going to bed is probably a better idea. Tomorrow we make our journey to the desert. Maybe we'll have a flash of clarity in the car. As I sink down into the comfy Mamounia bed, I'm wondering why anyone thinks sleeping in a tent is a good idea.

Chapter 10

"Are you sure you know how to drive this?

Olivia is perched on the edge of the front seat of our pale green Peugeot. Even at this early hour of the morning, the traffic at the airport is chaotic and driving out of the rental car area is going to be a challenge, but I'm not going to tell that to my friend.

"Piece of cake," I assure her. "We'll be on our way in a few minutes."

Olivia looks doubtful. "This is a stick shift. Have you ever driven one?"

"A long time ago, but it's like riding a bike—you never forget."

I press down on the clutch and put the car in gear. I'm not sure which gear since there are no markings anywhere, but as long as it's not reverse, we're good. When I gingerly step on the gas and attempt to let the clutch out, the car jerks forward a few feet and stalls. I glance at Olivia, who's holding onto the dashboard and muttering under her breath.

"No problem," I say. "I just have to get used to the vehicle."

It takes a bit for me to do that, but on the third try I manage to get the car going, and we lurch out of the parking lot and into traffic. We jerk spastically until I realize the clutch won't engage until it is nearly all the way out, which means there is a fine line between moving and stalling. Olivia releases her grip on the dashboard and slouches down in the seat.

"I'm closing my eyes now. Let me know if we make it out of the city without getting killed. And remind me again why we aren't traveling with the others. It seems to me that would have been a very smart decision."

The "others" are friends of Kadem who are joining us on our Sahara adventure. They're riding to our destination in a luxury SUV, but Olivia and I thought it would be fun to explore Morocco by ourselves. We can stop when we want to, and best of all, we don't have to chat with folks we don't know.

The traffic is horrendous, and signal lights don't seem to mean much. Cars whiz through red and stop on green. When I glance at Olivia, her eyes are closed, and she's holding her head. By the time I navigate the unfamiliar streets of Marrakech and head out of the city without getting clobbered by other vehicles, I'm beginning to feel confident. I've got this shifting thing under control and am actually having a bit of fun.

I thump Olivia on the leg. "This is super. Our adventure begins."

"Please watch the road," she mutters. "Don't talk and drive."

I feel myself relax as I look out the window. The sun is up, and the scenery is gorgeous. We drive past groves of olive trees and blooming oleander bushes. In front of us are the sunbathed peaks of the High Atlas mountains.

I open my window and inhale deeply. "Smell that air, Olivia. You don't get that in Wake Forest."

She peers through her fingers. “We have air in Wake Forest. Don’t inhale. Just concentrate on driving.”

“You’re missing a lot,” I tell her. I know I sound smug, but I can’t help it. I’m still astounded I managed to get the car through Marrakech traffic without getting both of us killed.

As we head into the Atlas mountains, the verdant landscape of the Marrakech area changes. The narrow two-lane road winds up through miles of brown sand and very little vegetation—or people. We pass a shepherd with his flock of sheep and a man slowly walking next to a donkey laden with bundles of straw. The steep road has no guardrail, and the few times I’m brave enough to look down I see the remains of cars that hurtled over the side and splatted far below. This was a fun adventure when we started out, but now I long to stop. My arms hurt from clutching the steering wheel, and my eyes are scratchy from staring at the road. As we climb up the mountain, the curves become sharper and the distance to the bottom distressingly far.

Suddenly Olivia screams, “Look out!” and points to a dusty pickup truck flying down the mountain, bouncing on the rutted road. Olivia screams again and buries her face in her hands. I fight off the urge to do the same and swerve to the right, praying we avoid a head on collision. The car begins to skid on the dirt and gravel, and I know we’re dangerously close to going over the edge.

The truck hurtles past us, and for a few minutes we sit there, stunned into silence. When I look down, I see we’re inches from joining the wrecked cars in the valley below.

Olivia exhales loudly. “Boy, that was close.”

“It sure was. I don’t suppose you’d like to drive.”

“You suppose correctly.” She pats my arm. “You’re doing a fine job.”

This is no longer fun, and now I wish we’d driven with the

others. I put the car in gear and drive slowly up the mountain. I'm concentrating so hard, I don't see the car behind us until our Peugeot lurches without any help from me. I look in the rearview mirror and am shocked to see a large black car on our bumper. And I mean right on our bumper.

"What the heck? What's that idiot doing?" The black car taps us again—this time with more force—and I feel my head snap back.

Olivia swivels around to see what's going on. "What's happening? Why is that car on our tail? Does it want to pass?"

"No idea." I stick my arm out the window and motion for the car to come around us. It responds by hitting us again.

"I don't think it wants to pass."

"Well, do something!" Olivia screeches. "He's going to force us off the road."

I stomp down on the gas, but if I'm expecting a burst of speed, I don't get it. The Peugeot has no git up and go, and maintains its sedate speed up the mountain. I try hugging the right side of the road, hoping the car will pass, but it hugs the right side with us.

Olivia has pulled out her cell phone and is frantically trying to make a call. "There's no service here. How are we supposed to get help?"

Now my palms are sweaty, and my hands keep slipping off the steering wheel. I search the road for a place to turn off, but don't see any. What does this person behind us want? We don't have any money, and we certainly aren't driving a fancy car. But this doesn't feel random. It's as if someone knows us and is deliberately trying to scare us—or worse.

Suddenly the black car is next to us, so close it clips the side mirror of the Peugeot. Olivia and I scream, and I automatically swerve to the right.

"Watch out!" Olivia yells. "He's trying to kill us."

I slam on the brakes, which the black car isn't expecting, and it roars up the narrow road and stops about fifty yards away.

"Let's get out of the car," I say to Olivia. "If we have to face these people I'd rather not be sitting down."

My legs are having trouble working and my heart is pounding like a jackhammer. I look up the road and see the black car is slowly backing down to us. It idles about twenty feet away, but there's no sign of its occupants. Olivia pokes me in the ribs.

"Look. A window's opening."

"I see that." And suddenly I have a plan. There's no cell phone service out here, but on the outside chance the folks in the car think we possess some kind of high tech, magical device, I begin to talk in a loud voice. I hold my cell phone to my ear and say, "If you could come right away, that would be awesome. Yes, we do have a weapon. Olivia, would you please fetch our weapon?"

She looks at me as if I have a screw loose. "Fetch? Our weapon?"

I nod. "Yes. The one in the car. You'll find it in my bag. Remember? We brought it from North Carolina."

I'm praying she'll remember our last-minute purchase at the airport. It takes her a second, but the lightbulb above her head lights up. She dives back into the car, plunges her hand into my bag and pulls out a silver fire starter shaped like a pistol. We bought it in case we need to start fires somewhere.

"Thank you, Olivia." I hold it at my side like a gun-toting moll from the wild west. "Yes, I have my weapon," I say into the phone. "And it's loaded. What should I do now? Hmm, I see." I look at the black car. "I understand. My friend's filming this now in case I have to shoot."

Olivia takes the hint and points her phone in the direction of the car. "Yes, I can give you the license number."

I start to walk slowly to the car, wondering what I'll do if I actually have to confront someone, but to my vast relief, I see the window close and the car silently move away.

I realize I've been holding my breath and let it out in one long woosh. I should have kept the air in my lungs because now I can't take a deep breath. As I sit on the ground gasping for air, Olivia is busy throwing up into a pile of dirt. I feel as miserable as she does, but this won't do. We have to get out of here. I force myself to calm down and breathe normally. I stand up and lurch over to Olivia.

"Are you okay? Let's get going. I've had enough."

"I couldn't agree with you more. What on earth was that all about."

"I don't know. Probably some jerk in a big car having fun."

There's no point telling Olivia right now what I really think. I have to have time to sort it out myself.

The road down the mountain is a twisting spiral of wicked curves, and by the time we reach the bottom, I'm limp as a wet noodle. We reach Skoura just in time. A few more minutes behind the wheel and I'd be a blubbering lump of exhaustion.

Chapter 11

There are three other couples waiting at the little restaurant. Two of them are French and seem pleasant enough, but they don't speak much English. After telling them our names and saying *Je suis une Americaine*, there isn't much more I can contribute. And Olivia is still traumatized and doesn't want to talk.

I'm astonished to see Corey Fieldstone and his wife. As I'm getting our things out of the car, he bounds over and shakes my hand vigorously. "Imagine us being on the same little trek to the desert. It was wonderful of Kadem to arrange this trip. It's going to be great fun."

I'm trying to imagine where Corey thought he was going when he got dressed this morning. He's wearing camo shorts, a white tank top, leather boots and a wide brim safari hat. A leather pouch tied to his waist contains what appears to be a knife and a water bottle. His wife, quiet as ever, is more suitably dressed in tan pants and a long sleeve white shirt.

"Didn't you see the memo, Corey?" I ask. "We're supposed to wear long pants for the camel ride. Something about chafing in the wrong places. And your skin will fry in that tank top."

"Don't worry about me. I've done several survival trips to dangerous places." He pats the pouch at his side. "I have everything I need."

"Okee dokee. I hope your wife has packed some aloe vera because you're going to need it."

A smiling man with a thick black moustache herds us together and claps his hands for attention. "Hello to all of you. I am Omar and I will be your guide in the desert. We will have an exciting adventure. Now please get into these vehicles." He points to four Land Rovers. "Two people in each car."

Olivia and I quickly hop into the vehicle nearest us. I'm so relieved that the hair-raising trip from Marrakech is over, I'm ready to relax and have a bit of fun.

"This is going to be awkward," Olivia says. "It appears Corey and what's-her-name are going to be our only social contacts."

I begin to laugh. "You can't think of her name, either, can you?"

She frowns. "I'm beginning to wish we weren't here. I may be forced to be sociable in French. That will leave you with your new friend and what's-her-name."

Not an appealing thought, but it's hard to be in a bad mood as we drive toward the Sahara.

"Can you believe we're doing this?" I say to Olivia.

"We're not in Wake Forest anymore. That's for sure. And all that drama in Marrakech seems far away." She adjusts her sunglasses and wraps a scarf around her head. "I don't need sand in my hair."

This makes me smile. "You do know we're going camping in the desert. There's a good chance you'll have sand in lots of other places."

She gives me a look. “We won’t be sitting in the sand, will we?”

I have to admit I don’t know. I’ve secretly been hoping “camping in a tent” is Kettani speak for luxury hotel.

“Kind of strange Corey and his wife are on this trip,” Olivia says. “I honestly don’t believe he was Peter’s great buddy. If he had been, we would have known him.”

“I think I have his number,” I tell her. “He’s trying hard to establish himself as a friend of the family. Sort of like a social climber back home. He probably told Kadem he’d always wanted to visit the Sahara desert, even if that’s not true. His motive might be doing more business deals with the Kettani empire or maybe he simply wants to be included in more social events. I think he’s harmless—a bit annoying but harmless.” I want to ask her something else. “You don’t suppose Mal could possibly be involved in any of this, do you?”

Olivia’s eyebrows rise above her sunglasses. “Why do you ask that? Have you noticed something?”

“Well, remember when we were in the kitchen talking to Suad, and Mal came in? Everyone got quiet, and I saw several ladies bow their heads and exchange glances.”

Olivia pulls two power bars and a bag of chips out of her bag and offers me some. “Maybe they behaved that way because Mal is part of the family, and as such they don’t trust her. We know she’s a down to earth, considerate, honest person, but they may not.”

“True,” I say. “I just have the feeling she somehow has enemies there. For instance, I don’t think Vivian likes her very much, and Vivian is a strong figure in that house.” I pause. “I just hope she isn’t in any danger.”

Olivia finishes the chips and licks salt off her fingers. “Answer me this. What if Mal is involved in something shady?”

She sees the look on my face and hastily adds, “I don’t mean killing Abdul. I mean, what if she really does need money. Would she resort to theft?”

This idea horrifies me. “Are you talking about stealing the ring? That’s ridiculous. She’d never do that, but even if she did steal it, she wouldn’t have a way to sell it. According to what Mal told us, it’s too well known, and I don’t think our pal would know how to contact any underground people.”

Olivia looks out the window. “There’s something going on there, Julia. The police are treating Abdul’s death as a robbery in the street gone bad. But what if the knife Suad showed us really is the knife that killed him? That means there probably is a dangerous person in the house. And I hate to say this, but what if our recent adventure on the road wasn’t simply due to a reckless driver? What if someone was intentionally trying to…well…kill us?”

So she and I are thinking the same thing. “But why would someone do that? We’re guests here. We don’t know most of these people. It did occur to me that our encounter with the black car may not have been accidental, but I don’t think the intention was to kill us. I think it was to scare us badly, and if that was the goal…well, mission accomplished.”

We both fall silent for the rest of the trip. I’d like to say I was mentally solving the mystery in Marrakech, but actually I was thinking about Dirk and wishing he were here and we were both somewhere far, far away.

The dunes are golden in the late afternoon sun, and the vastness of the desert is overwhelming. I immediately lose my sense of direction and wonder how our driver knows where he’s going. There’s nothing but undulating dunes as far as the eye can see—no vegetation, no people, nothing. I feel very small, and the camels we're approaching look very big.

I nudge Olivia. "Can you believe this? We're in the Sahara Desert."

"I can believe it. Sand is sticking to my lip gloss. Are we seriously going to get on those animals?"

"Looks that way, my friend."

The Land Rover stops, we all get out and our driver grins broadly. "You come here now," he says to me. "This one is for you." He points to a huge beast chewing something with big yellow teeth. He utters a command, touches the animal's chest and the camel drops to its knees. "You get on now."

Olivia, who has been watching, whispers in my ear. "You have fun. I'll be going."

"I don't think so. Look." The vehicles are slowly moving away.

Our driver misinterprets the panicked look on Olivia's face. "Please do not worry about the luggage. The cars are taking it to the camp. Please get on your camel."

There's nothing we can do. I try to console my friend. "Look at this as an exciting adventure. We sure couldn't do this in Wake Forest."

"Wake Forest is exactly where I wish I could be right now," she retorts. "Wake Forest doesn't have camels. This is just plain silly. These creatures smell."

Corey and his wife have already mounted their camels. "Super, isn't this?" he yells. "Absolutely amazing."

I try to ignore him as I consider the mechanics of mounting a camel. This beast is very high off the ground and has a considerable girth. And he doesn't look friendly. Our guide says to simply get on, sit on the blanket, grab the handle in front and lean back because camels rise first on their back legs. Then lean forward as the front legs come up. I do as I'm told and soon I'm gingerly straddling a camel.

As we get moving there's a lot of rocking and swaying involved and pain in the nether region, but I'm proud of myself. I'm actually riding a camel, and I'm beginning to enjoy myself. This sure wasn't on my bucket list, but maybe it should have been. Pretty soon I'm even able to loosen my death grip on the handle and put one hand in my lap, like someone who is blasé about riding camels. I'd like to say I'm brave, but it has more to do with the fact that I saw all the animals are tethered together. Mine couldn't run away if it wanted to. I swivel my head to look at Olivia behind me and give her a thumb's up. She scowls and gives me a different finger.

Eventually, Omar, who's riding the first camel, points to dark dots in the distance and yells, "Tents." As we draw closer I see four beige tents with their flaps open and a larger tent several yards away. It's amazing Kadem has created this little oasis in the middle of the desert, and it's all staffed and cared for by his employees. I can well imagine visiting dignitaries are delighted to accept an exciting trip to the Sahara.

When we reach the camp, our camels once again kneel, we dismount, and Omar gives instructions. "Here are the tent assignments. Tent One is for the ladies." He smiles at me. "The second for Fieldstone, third is for DuBois and fourth is for Boucher. The dining tent is the large tent over there," he says, pointing. "There are two toilette tents behind here. Tents One and Two share Valley of the Roses, and Three and Four will share the Pineapple Broom Tree. The names are on the tents."

Olivia does not look happy. "Does this mean what I think it means? We're sharing a "toilette" tent with the folks next door? I don't think so, Julia. Let's go find a nice hotel."

I tend to agree with her, but unfortunately there's no nice hotel within miles. We're going to have to pretend we enjoy rustic, outdoor facilities. I try to be optimistic. "Maybe it won't be so bad. I'll bet we'll be pleasantly surprised." Even I don't believe my words.

I walk over to our tent and step inside. This doesn't look so bad. There are two cots with heavy colorful blankets, a red, purple and green Berber rug on the ground and a bag hanging on a rope from the top of the tent. There is also a small wooden table with two bottles of water. And our small duffle bags are in the corner.

I pull my laptop out of my bag, put it on the table and go out to find Omar. "Everything is very nice, but what's the bag on a rope for?"

"That's for your food or valuables, madam. Animals sometimes visit the tents at night. It is better to keep things off the ground."

Olivia, who is listening, says, "What kind of animals, Omar? I have to know what we're dealing with here."

Omar seems uncomfortable. "Small desert animals, madam. Not to worry."

"I repeat. What kind of animals."

"Sometimes snakes or lizards, but do not worry, madam. They will not come."

"Why won't they come? What do we do if I suddenly see a snake trying to climb up my bed?"

I try to pull Olivia away. "Leave it alone. There's nothing we can do." Except maybe stay awake all night with something heavy in our hands—but I didn't say that out loud.

We're almost in our tent when Corey stops us. "Isn't this a marvelous place? Wonderful for some serious meditation. How do you like your accommodations?" He puts an arm around each of our shoulders and peers inside. "Primitive but wonderful. Kadem did an amazing job creating this place. We'll have many memories to take home."

He's inside and looking around before I realize it. "Yes, primitive but functional. I see you've brought your laptop, Julia. You know that won't work here. And only two small duffel bags? I thought ladies traveled with lots of luggage."

I shake his arm off my shoulder. "You have a wife, Corey. She's a lady. Doesn't she have luggage?"

"Well, of course she does. She brought a proper piece, though. Not a tiny little bag. You seem so antagonistic, Julia."

"We're only here for two nights," I remind him. "Now, if you wouldn't mind, Olivia and I have to get organized. See you later, Corey."

He's still talking as I close the flap.

Chapter 12

The food is simple but tasty and served buffet style. Tajines of chicken and vegetables and platters of fruit. I recognize two men and one woman working in the dining tent as employees at the Kettani home.

Olivia and I are sitting at a long table with the other guests, and I'm having a hard time trying to chat with the Bouchers. If they speak any English, they're not letting on, and I've exhausted the few words of French I know. Olivia, however, is chattering away, so I tune out and concentrate on eating. I'm almost relieved when Corey and Belle sit down next to me.

"Isn't this the greatest place? Such an adventure. The folks back home will never believe my stories."

"Speaking of folks back home, Corey—where is home? I don't think you ever told us."

He reaches across the table to take a mango from the platter. "I'm from a little town not far from Pittsburgh. Growing up was pretty dull. I did the usual stuff; played football, fixed my car, things like that. No excitement."

Corey's body reminds me of a fat beetle, so the football thing surprises me. "It sounds like you've come a long way for a small-town boy. Are you also in international banking?"

He looks amused. "More import/export."

I take a bite of delicious roasted eggplant. "What do you import?"

His expression changes from amused to annoyed. "You sure do have a lot of questions."

"Just trying to fill in the blanks," I say innocently. "Mal and Peter are good friends so I'm wondering why we never saw you in Chapel Hill."

"I'm assuming you weren't with them twenty-four hours a day. I'm sure they had friends you don't know about."

Now he's sounding downright snarky, and I should stop talking, but common sense is sometimes not one of my virtues. "Where did you stay when you visited Chapel Hill?"

I can see he's debating his answer. If he says hotel, he knows I'll ask which one, and if he says he stayed with Mal and Peter, I'll know he's not telling the truth because they had a studio apartment. No guest accommodations. He solves the problem by abruptly standing up and saying, "It's been a long day. Time for bed."

He leaves the dining tent in such a hurry he forgets his wife, who's still eating.

"Why are you poking the bear?" Olivia asks. "He obviously didn't like your questions."

"I don't know. I guess he gets to me because he's trying to claw his way into a friendship with Mal and Peter. I'd be willing to bet he somehow managed to tell Kadem that he and Peter are besties. Kadem, being a busy man, never gave it a second thought and probably never mentioned it to his son. So Corey is managing to weasel his way into social—and perhaps business—

functions with the Kettanis."

"And why do you care about that?"

"I just do. I don't like phony people."

"It's really none of our business, is it?"

I hate it when Olivia decides to be logical. I'm about to give her a lecture on false friends when I notice one of the ladies on the kitchen staff looking at me. She inclines her head to the left and then looks back at me. I interpret this to mean she wants to talk so I tell Olivia I'll be right back and casually wander to the kitchen door.

I'm standing almost next to her, but she continues to wipe the counter and doesn't look up. Instead she says softly, "You in danger. Have to go."

I have no idea what she means, but her words are enough to start a turmoil in my stomach. "What danger? How do you know?"

She keeps wiping, her eyes on the counter. "Go. No talk."

"Please tell me one thing. Were you in the kitchen with Suad when I was there?"

Her nod is almost imperceptible as she moves away.

Night falls heavily in the desert, and it's black as ink when we step outside and head to our tent. No streetlights, no house lights and still too early for the moon.

"Thank heavens we have our phones," Olivia says as she turns on the flashlight. Otherwise we wouldn't be able to see a thing."

I suddenly stop walking. "I forgot to charge mine before we left, and I sure can't charge it here. I'm glad you have yours because I don't think I've ever seen night so dark."

I'm relieved when we reach our tent and are safely inside.

Something doesn't feel right. I use the flashlight on Olivia's cell phone to look around the little room. "I think someone has been in here. I left my bag near the foot of my cot. Now it's over there. And everything has fallen out of my cosmetic bag." My bracelet's on the ground, and I find the pendant I bought in the souk under my bed.

"Maybe a rat did this." Olivia sits down on her cot. "This is not my idea of fun."

"It's not mine either, but Kadem is trying to do something exciting and different for his guests." I decide not to tell her what the woman in the dining tent said. There's no reason for both of us to be nervous wrecks.

We decide to sleep in our clothes in case we have to exit our tent rapidly. I'd love to wash my face and brush my teeth, but we only have half a bottle of water between us. Too late we remembered being told to pick up extra bottles at dinner. Now I'm very thirsty, and my mouth is so parched I think my lips are cracking. The desert air must be extra dry. I can't fall asleep because the blanket is heavy and scratchy and too hot. If I kick it off, I'm too cold. For a while I try diagraming sentences in my mind—a favorite soporific—and when that doesn't work, I whisper to Olivia, thinking we can chat for a bit, but she's snoring softly. Now I have to go to the bathroom. I try using positive thoughts to convince me to ignore the urge, but that also isn't working—and it is not wise to wait too long.

I think it's around 2:00 a.m. when I get up and tiptoe out of the tent. The moon is up and is bathing the sand in a silver light so I'm able to see where I'm going. And there are a million stars in the sky. I walk carefully to the toilet tent, praying no one else is using it at this hour.

Whoever named this place the Valley of the Roses had a sense of humor because it definitely is not, and the toilet itself wouldn't win any home décor award. It's a hollowed-out piece of wood with two strips of stone for a seat. I have a vision of my hindquarters freezing to the cold seat, thereby necessitating an embarrassing removal procedure and decide to forego sitting.

When I leave the toilet tent a cloud has moved across the moon making the night once again pitch black. I move cautiously in what I hope is the right direction. It's a strange sensation to walk in the dark across sand without any kind of landmark or familiar anchor. I'm wondering how sightless people relearn their world when a hand roughly grabs my arm and another hand is slapped across my mouth before I can scream. A man's low voice growls something I don't understand.

I'm beyond terrified, but a survival instinct takes over and I struggle to get free. I twist around to see my captor, but he's wearing a scarf over his head and face so only his eyes are visible, and I can't see them in the dark. I aim a kick at his leg and hear him wince in pain. But he doesn't let go. He smells of camel and tobacco. I fight as hard as I can to get away from him, but he's too strong. And he's apparently tired of dealing with me because he clonks me on the side of my forehead with something heavy, and the next think I know I'm lying on my back and there's sand all over me.

When I open my eyes, I see stars, but thankfully they're the ones in the sky and not in my head. The side of my forehead hurts, though, and my fingers are sticky when I touch it. Blood. Blood and sand can't be a healthy combination, so I stagger to my feet and lurch to our tent, which is thankfully only a few feet away.

Once inside I stand at the foot of Olivia's bed and grab her feet. "Help! I need some water."

Olivia bolts upright, and there's a lot of clatter as she reaches for her phone, drops it in the dark, finally locates it and switches on the flashlight. And gasps.

"You're bleeding. Do you know that? It's dripping all over the place. What on earth happened? Did you fall? We need to wash that. Lordy, there's sand everywhere. Why were you outside? I thought we agreed we'd go to the toilet tent together."

I wait until she runs out of words and then say, "Someone clonked me on the head. It was a very deliberate attack, and as soon as the sun comes up, I'm leaving."

She looks worried as she examines my head. "We need to wash that." She reaches for our half bottle of water, soaks a wad of toilet paper and dabs at my head. "This may need stitches, Julia, or at least a butterfly bandage. It's a good thing I came prepared."

She opens a bag and begins to pull out first aid supplies. I back away. "There's no way I'm letting you sew my head."

"Relax. I have antibiotic ointment and a butterfly bandage. My goodness, head wounds certainly do bleed, don't they? I'm afraid this blanket is ruined. Here, take these," she says handing me two pills. "I got them for pain when I had oral surgery, and they work fast. Do you think we should wake up Omar and tell him what happened?"

"I definitely do not. I don't know where he sleeps, and he might be alarmed when the two of us appear in the middle of the night. We'll sit tight until morning."

But I can't sit tight. I try. I honestly do. I try to sit quietly and think of a happy place, but at the moment the only happy place is my house in Wake Forest, which is far, far away. Thinking about it makes my eyes fill with tears. Olivia has patched me up with the butterfly bandage, but my heart is still pounding from terror, and every inch of my body is quivering. I have to get out. Now.

"Grab your stuff, Olivia. We're leaving."

"Right now? Where are we going? And how are we going to get out of here?"

"I don't know, but we'll think of something."

"Are you sure? Doesn't your head hurt?"

"Now that you mention it, not so much. I'm good to go. Just thinking about leaving this place makes me feel better."

Fortunately we didn't unpack because there's no place to put things, so we're out of the tent in a few minutes. I'm happy to see the clouds are gone and the bright moon makes walking on the sand easy. I look up at the moon and see it's swaying slightly. I've never seen that before, but maybe it's a Sahara phenomenon.

"Where are we going?" Olivia asks. "I don't understand how we're going to get out of here."

"Leave that to me, little lady."

"Excuse me? Little lady? Are you feeling okay?"

"Actually, I am. You're swaying, too. Why can't you stand still? And your voice sounds mushy."

"Oh boy," I hear her say. "I think the pills I gave you are making you loony. Maybe we should go back."

"Not on your life. I'm good, and I've found our transportation."

"You have?"

"I have, indeed. Have a look."

Olivia shines the flashlight into the darkness. "Where? I only see the camels tethered for the night."

I rub my hands together. "Exactly. We'll steal one and ride away."

She shines the flashlight onto my face. "Let me see your eyes. I think you're concussed. We're not stealing camels. What on earth are you thinking?"

"I'm thinking this is a good idea." Although at the moment I'm not so sure. Her voice is so fuzzy, and now the camels are swaying. I step in front of the first one and look him/her in the eye. Could it be a her? I peer closely at the face and see long eyelashes, so it must be a girl. This is good. It's probably easier to reason with a girl camel.

From some distant place I hear Olivia say, "Don't stand in front of a camel. I understand they can spit, and the spit is very unpleasant."

She sounds so funny—almost as if she's speaking with marbles in her mouth. "Olivia, can you please speak French and tell this camel to sit. She probably doesn't understand English. But first lose whatever you have in your mouth."

"Please, Julia, get away from there."

When the camel fails to sit, I thump it on the chest as I saw Omar do earlier.

"Julia! Don't do that!"

She doesn't sit. In fact, now she's tilting to the right. So are the dunes. I have to tilt my head to see them, and that suddenly hurts. My eyeballs hurt. I feel Olivia next to me, and this time I can hear her much better.

"Come with me. There's a Land Rover over there, and we're going to take it. You're not okay, Julia. We have to get you to a doctor."

"I'm fine," I protest, but I know I'm not. We reach the vehicle, and miraculously it's unlocked. I sit down in the passenger seat while Olivia searches for the keys. Now my head is throbbing, and I feel like I'm going to throw up. I glance over at my friend, who is frantically searching through the side pocket on the door.

"Look on the tire," I manage to say.

"What? Look where?"

"On the top of the tire. My uncle used to hide his keys there," I tell her—right before I pass out.

By the time we reach Skoura, Aziz is waiting to take us back to Marrakech. Olivia has called Mal and told her what happened. She could have left out the part about me wanting to steal a camel, but I guess in the interest of accuracy, she had to reveal all. And Mal is absolutely insisting we stay at her house. She talked about nourishing food, good medical care and other things I can't remember. My head hurts too much to argue with her. Hopefully tomorrow will be a better day.

Chapter 13

"We absolutely insist. It's not open for discussion. Kadem is horrified this happened."

Mal flutters around me adjusting pillows and smoothing the duvet. I'm lying in an ornately carved bed on what must be a million thread count sheets in a room fit for a palace. And Olivia is in an equally luxurious connecting room.

"Kadem wants you to stay here until your head is all better. The doctor said you need rest."

I try to bat her hand away. "I promise you I'm fine, and this is totally unnecessary."

The Kettani doctor has examined my wound, rebandaged it, looked in my eyes and pronounced me healthy but slightly concussed. He said a period of rest would be a good idea, and now I'm trying to convince Mal that doesn't mean I have to stay in bed. Rest means no marathon running. I intend to get up as soon as she leaves.

She perches on the foot of the bed. "I can't believe this happened to you. And at our Sahara camp. Who would do such a thing? Kadem thinks it must have been a marauding thief—someone who knew about the camp and was looking for something to steal."

I don't agree, but I need more time to think. I don't believe it was random. The person who clobbered me didn't steal anything and didn't try to assault anyone else in the camp. It was another attempt to scare me.

I'm dying to ask Mal to finish what she was trying to tell me when we had coffee at La Mamounia but am not sure this is the right time. I say this because the twitch under her eye has started again, and this time it's so visible I can't help staring at it.

"I hope you know you can always talk to me," I say. "I feel fine and am ready to listen."

"Is it that visible?" She tries to laugh, but it sounds more like a groan. "There are some things going on here that I really don't understand."

"Like what?"

"Well, for instance, I think someone has been following me when I go out."

"How can that be? Aziz is always with you."

She turns to look at me, and I'm shocked to see how stressed she seems. "Aziz says I'm imagining it, but I know I'm not. It's a man with a hat pulled down low over his head, and he's always wearing a dirty blue jacket and black pants. If I turn around quickly to catch a glimpse of him, he ducks into doorways or behind cars. One time I pretended to use my powder compact and watched him in the mirror. He caught on to what I was doing and disappeared into the crowd. I know I'm not imagining it." Her voice fades. "I have to admit I'm a bit scared."

"This is awful. Have you told Peter or Kadem? Surely they

could put a stop to this."

"Kadem and Peter are totally consumed with a possible big business deal. And they're both flying to Paris this afternoon. I don't want to bother them."

I get out from under the duvet and crawl down the bed to sit next to her. "Please don't be upset. Is everything okay between you and Peter? I only ask because you don't seem happy, and you said you want to go back to Wake Forest. I know moving here was a big adjustment, and it's understandable if you're having trouble."

She shakes her head. "No, it's not that. I love Peter and he loves me. He told me the other day he doesn't want to stay here permanently. Working with his father was worth a try, but he also misses North Carolina."

"I'm glad to hear that. So let's do something about the jerk following you. Olivia and I will help. We're good at this stuff."

She smiles weakly and puts her hand on my knee. "You're concussed. Remember? You're supposed to be resting."

"Honestly, Mal, I'm fine, and I hate to see you this way. You've been so kind to us, and now we'll do everything we can to help you."

"Kadem would be angry if I let you leave before the doctor okays it. He's coming to recheck you at the end of the week."

"Then let's do this. If it's okay with you I'll stay here until the doc releases me, But I feel fine and certainly don't have to stay in bed. Let's try to figure out what the guy following you is doing. And don't worry," I say, seeing the look on her face, "there will be three of us and one of him. What can possibly go wrong?"

Mal finally kisses me on the forehead and leaves, but not before saying, "If you want anything—anything at all—just pick up the house phone and ask. We want you to be comfortable."

As soon as she closes the door, I bounce out of bed and instantly regret it. The posh room begins to spin, and I have to sit down. Olivia opens the connecting door and comes in.

"I knew you wouldn't stay in bed. Are we going to get out of here? I'm already feeling confined."

I study my friend carefully. She's trying to behave normally, but she looks extremely nervous.

"So what's up? Anything you want to tell me?

She stares at the ceiling and then the floor. "I may have done something that's going to upset you."

I narrow my eyes and give her my best steely glare. "And what would that be?"

"I may have accidentally told Oliver about your unfortunate incident in the desert. And he may have told Dirk, and Dirk may have called me wanting details. He told Oliver he'd been calling your cellphone over and over and hasn't been able to reach you. Oliver said he sounds frantic."

My cellphone! In all the confusion I'd totally forgotten to charge it. To be honest, I hadn't even thought about it.

"Anyway, Dirk is very worried about you and is coming sooner than planned. They both are. They'll be here at the end of the week. Please don't be mad at me, Julia. You should know we're all concerned about you."

I'm secretly happy to hear Dirk will be here soon. He's a solid, wonderful, caring, strong man, and I could really use one of those right now. And handsome. I almost forgot handsome. He came into my life quite accidentally. My husband, Tony, had been dead for two years, and when I finally felt like living again, Olivia and I planned a trip to Iceland. A romantic involvement was the last thing on my mind. But Dirk was a passenger on that trip, and there was an instant spark between us.

Lightning struck Olivia the same way. She and I were

attending a conference for small restaurant owners on Hilton Head Island. Oliver Parker-Smythe arrived in his magnificent yacht to buy a priceless book. Olivia had three failed marriages behind her and had sworn off men for good. And then along came Oliver.

When Olivia realizes I'm not mad, she says, "So should we get out of here now? I'm already feeling confined."

I wince as I touch my head. "Maybe we should stay a bit longer." I tell her about Mal's stalker. "I'd like to help her, and if we stay here, we'll be able to do some snooping. I'd also like to find out who's trying to give me a heart attack—and why. Let's stay until Dirk and Oliver come. Maybe by then we'll have some answers."

"This sounds like a really bad idea, but I probably can't talk you out of it. If we're staying, we have to find something to eat. Aren't you starving?"

"I do feel a bit peckish—as my grandmother used to say. Mal said to use the house phone to call if I needed something, but let's find the kitchen—and see if we can find Suad. I'd rather eat there."

I've never been lost in a private home before, but there's a first time for everything. Olivia and I start down a long hall, and I could swear we're going the right way because I think I recognize two ornate, tall vases. When we near a room with an open door, we hear a voice and realize we're still in the bedroom wing and the voice we hear belongs to Vivian.

"I think everything is coming along quite well. I don't anticipate any problems. You do your part." There's a pause, then "Very good. See you this afternoon. You know I love you."

Olivia gives me a poke. "Do you hear that?" she whispers.

I pull her away. "I do. And she can't have been talking to

Kadem. She can't see him this afternoon. He's on his way to Paris."

We're so busy whispering about Vivian we almost run smack into a very muscular man wearing a tank top and jeans, who, when he sees us, quickly ends a call on his cellphone. And he doesn't look happy. He blocks our way and says, "Who are you, and what are you doing here?"

His accent is pure American, which makes me feel better. He's one of us. I stick out my hand. "I'm Julia Greene and this is my friend, Olivia. We're guests of Malika."

He ignores my hand and scowls. "Why wasn't I told?"

This person isn't being very pleasant. "I'm sure I don't know. Could you please move."

I have no idea who invited him here, but as far as I'm concerned, he's being rude and needs to leave us alone. I try to walk around him, but he sticks out his hand to stop me and bellows, "Vivian!" loud enough to wake up people in Casablanca.

Vivian comes out of her room and stops in her tracks when she sees us. "What's going on, Brandon?"

"I found these two wandering around here. I thought you'd want to know."

"We weren't wandering," I say defensively. "We were on our way to the kitchen. Who is this man?"

Vivian recovers from her surprise at seeing us and tries to be cordial. "This is Brandon. He's our security person here at the house. It's quite okay," she says to the man. "These ladies are guests of my daughter-in-law, although I'm not quite sure what you're doing here, Julia. Your room is the other way. And aren't you supposed to be in bed?"

"Nice seeing you, Vivian. If it's okay with you, we'll be going." This time when I attempt to walk past Brandon, he moves, and Olivia and I high tail it to the kitchen. When we finally find it we burst through the door as if our hair is on fire. Suad looks up from a soup she's stirring and smiles.

"You hungry? Want tea?"

"Yes, hungry. No tea. Is there any coffee?" I ask hopefully.

The kitchen isn't as crowded as it was the other night—probably because there's no party scheduled. Suad tells us to sit at the table and begins to ply us with wonderful breads and fried eggs with black olives, pancakes with a buttery honey syrup, delicious jams and coffee. She grins as she refills my cup.

"Is good?"

"It sure is. The whole breakfast is amazing." I stop eating for a second and say, "Olivia, can you ask her about the goon we just met in the hall. Who is Brandon?"

I can tell from the look on Suad's face she doesn't think much of the security person. "Apparently Vivian hired him not long ago," Olivia translates. "She said she was concerned about her safety here. Suad doesn't know where she found him, but he's obviously American. And he's been rough on the employees, bossing them around—as if he enjoys some favored status."

"He looks like a thug," I say. "I'm sure he wears those tank tops to display his muscles."

We eat until all the food is gone, and I feel ten pounds heavier. And then I remember another reason I wanted to come to the kitchen. "Olivia, could you ask Suad if we could see Abdul's room? Maybe there's a clue in there that everyone has missed."

I wait while the two have a brief conversation, and soon Suad walks to the kitchen door and motions for us to follow her to the staff quarters at the back of the house.

Abdul's room is clean and functional. There's a narrow bed with a colorful blanket, a wooden table and chair and a small Berber rug on the floor. I feel uneasy entering, probably because I'm remembering how the poor man died.

"I don't see any personal belongings," I say to Olivia. "There must have been photos or books. Could you please ask Suad what happened to them?"

I wait while the two confer. "She says Abdul's sister took all his personal belongings, and he didn't have very much. He had very few clothes and even fewer personal items. Everything but the clothes were in a small metal box."

Hmm. "Does Suad know what was in the box?"

"She says just little stuff, like a good luck charm and some things Fatima gave him." She pauses to listen to more. "Abdul drove and did other errands for Fatima for over ten years. He was totally devoted to her and was devastated when she got sick and died. He never seemed to get over her death."

"That's very sad. I can imagine it was hard for him to see her replaced. Did he drive for Vivian?"

Olivia asks the question and Suad shakes her head vigorously back and forth. "She says no way. Vivian had a new driver—someone brought in after she married Kadem."

It isn't hard to see that the new Mme. Kettani isn't very popular among the staff, or that the staff is upset the Kettani family seems to have forgotten about Abdul.

"Suad says Madam Kettani came to this room after Abdul was killed. The staff thought she'd come to help gather his things, but all she wanted to do was snoop around."

"Vivian did this? I wonder what she was looking for."

Suad appears to understand my question because she says, "*Pas Vivian. L'autre Mme. Kettani.*"

The other Madam Kettani? Malika? What in the world would she be looking for here?

Chapter 14

"Are you sure they aren't home? I'd hate to get caught doing this." Olivia burps delicately. "That breakfast sure was good."

"I'm positive. Mal is away until early evening working on a charity event. I saw her get in the car and drive away with Aziz. Vivian is spending the afternoon at a spa, and Kadem and Peter are on their way to Paris. We have plenty of time, so let's do this." I've convinced Olivia to search the former master bedroom with me.

"And we're trespassing here because…?"

"It's very simple. I think the solution to everything somehow lies with Fatima. Abdul was her driver and confidante. Did he know something that possibly got him killed? Mal and Fatima had a special relationship, and Mal is obviously stressed about something. Vivian told me she saw Mal come out of Fatima's room. What was she doing in there? Is she in danger? We have to find out."

We also have to stop talking because we hear footsteps on the other side of the door. "Quick," I say. "Someone's coming out of the room. We have to hide."

But there's no suitable place. The only things in the hall are two enormous cloisonné vases. Olivia and I each scurry behind one and crouch down. And just in time. The door to the room opens and Brandon comes out. He pulls the door shut with more force than necessary and strides down the hall.

"That was close. Maybe we shouldn't do this." Olivia anxiously scans the hall. "What if he comes back?"

"Don't worry. He was probably just doing his security thing." I sound confident, but I don't feel that way.

I have to pick the lock—a skill I developed on our trip to Iceland. It's amazing what you can do with two long hairpins. When I hear the lock click, I take a deep breath and open the door. The room smells musty with a faint hint of roses. This used to be the master bedroom and at one time was a splendid example of Moroccan décor—heavy drapes, mosaic tiles and marble. Even though Vivian has removed many furnishings, the room almost vibrates with color. Porcelain purple and green birds sit on a golden footstool. Next to the footstool is a cherry red velvet chair. There's also a lovely sitting area with a pale lavender chaise, a low glass table with crystal glasses, and chairs upholstered in a pale lemon and peacock patterned silk. The bed has an elaborately carved headboard and a pale lavender duvet. Fatima must have been an energetic, happy person. Vivian, on the other hand, is British, much more reserved and seems fond of the color brown.

Someone has searched the room thoroughly. In the enormous closet, drawers have been pulled open and the contents thrown on the ground. There are almost no clothes left but I step over an expensive looking gown and a pair of crystal studded evening shoes.

"Who would do this? Surely you can search for something

without ruining pretty clothes."

Olivia picks up a gorgeous sweater and shakes her head. "It's awful. Do you suppose Kadem knows about this?"

"He probably never comes in here. And it's obvious the staff isn't cleaning."

"Didn't Mal say Vivian was having all Fatima's belongings removed? Most of the clothes are gone, but there's a lot of stuff left."

I pick up papers lying on the floor in front of an antique desk. They seem to be invoices for purchases Fatima made and were obviously not interesting to the person who searched the room. I look in all the drawers, but aside from some expensive underwear, the drawers are empty. There's nothing here to help us, and that's disappointing. I don't know what I expected. I guess I thought Fatima might have left a clue.

Olivia heads to the door. "I'm leaving. I'm afraid we're going to be caught."

As she walks, her toe catches the corner of a small rug. The rug flips back, and I see a chain. "That's weird," I say as I move the rug away. "Why would there be a chain on the floor?" I give it a yank and pull up a square piece of wood. The wood was covering a hole in the ground, and the hole is full of things.

"This only happens in movies!" I exclaim, as I pull out the contents. There's a bank book in Fatima's name from a London bank, many letters written in Arabic and tied with a silk yellow ribbon, and Fatima's passport.

"Look at this," Olivia says. She's holding an envelope and what looks like a legal document. "This is written in French, and it's from an investigation agency. I can't understand all of it, but I see Kadem's name mentioned quite a few times. Maybe she was having her husband followed."

We write down the address of the agency. Maybe I'll be able

to think of a way to get more info from them.

There's more in the secret hole. I pick up a lovely antique doll. The lace on her dress has yellowed with age, and her patent leather shoe cracks when I touch it. She has soft brown hair and brown eyes that don't move. I wonder who owned the doll and why it has been carefully preserved all these years. As I put it back, my hand touches another object. It's a turquoise folder with a silver clip, and it was in Mal's hand the last time I saw it.

Olivia peers over my shoulder. "Is that what I think it is? What's it doing here?"

My hand is shaking as I open the folder and look at the contents. There's Abdul's driver's license and identity papers, another invoice from the investigation agency addressed to Mal, three newspaper articles about the Kettani ruby, and an appraisal of the ring dated seventeen months ago. The appraisal amount is in dirham, and there are an awful lot of zeros.

I sit down on the floor and show the appraisal document to Olivia. "This is addressed to Mme. Kettani, but it doesn't say which one. It was sent to this house, but that doesn't help because they both live here."

I return all the papers to the folder and place everything back in the hiding place. "You know," I say, "Mal hid this folder in here, so it's something she doesn't feel comfortable keeping in her room. And how does she happen to have Abdul's driver's license? And why? I sure wish I knew what was going on."

I avoid mentioning the articles about the Kettani Ruby because it makes my stomach queasy to think Mal might've had something to do with its disappearance. I wish I could ask her, but I'm pretty sure I know what her reaction would be if I tell her I picked the lock to the room, found her secret hiding place and looked at everything in it. And by the way, why did you have Abdul's papers, and did you steal the ruby? Nope. I'll have to figure this out by myself.

"We have to put all of this back and pretend we never saw it," I say.

"How can we do that?" Olivia objects. "Shouldn't we confront Mal and ask her what's going on?"

I replace the wood and smooth out the rug. "That isn't going to work. We'll have to think of something else."

"Julia," Olivia says as we head to our bedroom, "do you think Mal was involved in Abdul's murder? I mean, I know she didn't do it because she was with us when it happened, but…"

"Of course not. Our sweet Mal would never be involved in something like that. And the three of us were sitting by the pool when Suad came running across the lawn with the dreadful news."

But now that I think about it, I realize I don't know how long Abdul had been lying there. Perhaps he hadn't been freshly killed when we saw him. He wasn't on the driveway when we drove up with Aziz, but we'd waited nearly forty minutes for Mal to finish an important call before she greeted us. Was she really on the phone or… I push the unthinkable thought out of my head.

"I need fresh air," I say to Olivia. Let's go outside."

We decide to go through the kitchen rather than through the fancy rooms and out the massive front door. We're almost there when we run smack into Vivian, who's walking briskly and has a scowl on her face. I'm hoping she can't see the shock on my face because she's not supposed to be home yet. We were very nearly caught snooping in Fatima's room.

"What are you two doing?" she says when she sees us, then quickly remembers she's the gracious hostess. "The staff will be happy to bring you anything you need. I believe I told you that."

I nod. "You did, indeed. We're hoping to pick up a piece of

fruit in the kitchen and then go for a walk. No need to bother anyone."

As we talk, I give Vivian a once over. She sure doesn't look like she's been relaxing at a spa all day. Her face has splotchy red marks and her normal lacquered hair is a mess. She also seems extremely jittery.

"You've been so gracious having us here. I promise you we're leaving as soon as the doctor releases me."

This news appears to cheer her up. "Well, then. Enjoy your walk and I hope we'll see you later. Be sure to tell the staff if you require food or drink."

"Honestly," Olivia says as we push through the kitchen door, "that woman has the personality of a turtle. What on earth does Kadem see in her?"

"Good question. Maybe he was lonely after Fatima died and didn't want to be alone. But now that you mention it, I'm going to try to find out more about her when we get back to the room. I bet I'll find something on Google."

The kitchen is almost empty. I nod to a girl arranging a tea pot and glasses on a tray as we continue to the back door. The fresh air feels wonderful on my face.

"It's great to be out of there. It amazes me such a beautiful house can feel so much like a prison."

Olivia adjusts her sunglasses and nods. "I totally agree. I can't wait until we can leave"—she grins—"which will also mean Dirk and Oliver will be here."

"I haven't forgotten."

It will be wonderful to see him. I honestly never thought there could be anyone else in the world to love. Tony was my everything, and when he was killed, I was positive life was over. And for a while it seemed to be, but Olivia wouldn't allow me to fester in my misery. She insisted we take the trip to Iceland, and

I'm sure karma was at work, because Dirk was on the same trip. He had planned to treat his son to a wonderful Iceland experience, but at the last minute his son couldn't go. Dirk decided he needed a break from lawyering and kept his reservation. It was almost love at first sight, although I didn't realize it at the time. And then I almost wrecked everything by overthinking everything—we lived too far apart, he'd find someone younger and prettier—the whole stupid, insecure nonsense. But we got past that, and now we're in a good place. And soon he'll be here.

"Suad said the knife was found near Mal's bedroom," I say to Olivia. "That would be to the left and around the corner. Let's see if we can find something."

Even though I'm on a mission, it's hard to ignore the gorgeous landscaping. It must cost a fortune to keep this lush paradise in such splendid order. The mingled scents of blooming flowers and citrus trees are overwhelming. We stop at a particularly beautiful pale yellow rosebush, every petal absolutely perfect.

"It looks almost unreal," Olivia says brushing her finger across the blooms. "My roses don't look like that."

"Your flowers are great," I tell her, "and you're not spending a bazillion dollars to keep them that way."

About fifty yards from Mal's window, there's a small black bench on a patch of grass. Next to it, several broken branches of hibiscus flowers are on the ground, a jarring sight in a perfect garden. I bend down to pick up a wilted pink flower.

"This sure seems out of place. I wonder why the gardeners haven't thrown this away. Do you suppose Abdul and his attacker could have been here?"

Olivia looks doubtful. "They said he was attacked in the street and staggered up the drive."

I step off the grass and into an area with more broken

branches. This place also looks like it's been trampled—and there's a large glob of a reddish-brown substance on a leaf. And there's more of the stuff leading out of the dirt and onto the grass. Blood? My churning stomach seems to think so.

"I think maybe Abdul and his attacker might have fought here. This looks like blood."

Olivia shivers. "That doesn't make any sense, Julia. If he was stabbed here, why didn't he run into the house for help? He could have gone in the same way we came out, but instead he went to the driveway."

"I'll admit that doesn't make much sense. Maybe Abdul was only wounded here. He scuffled with the murderer, and when the person tried to get away, Abdul followed him to the driveway trying to stop him."

"So the murderer could be a stranger? A family member wouldn't run to the driveway. A family member would go in the house. And if the killer was back here in the garden, it can't have been a random thing. It means Abdul was deliberately targeted. But if a stranger killed him, how did he or she get the knife from the kitchen?"

"Good question. I'm very confused. Maybe the killer wasn't a stranger. Suad certainly believes it was an inside job. Whoever did it had to have been covered in blood, so he or she couldn't go back into the house and also couldn't run through the streets. The person had to go somewhere to ditch the clothes and wash off the blood."

"True," Olivia says, "but where?"

I look around the massive garden, wondering where someone would go to scrub away evidence of the crime. There's the swimming pool, a koi pond, and an elaborate fountain with water lilies at its base. The pool is out because it's too visible from the house, and we decide ditto the koi pond because that's just cruel to the poor fish. But the fountain is at the end of the rose garden on a secluded path. Mal told us Kadem had it built after Fatima died as almost a shrine to her. It makes me sick to think the killer desecrated it with his bloody clothes, but we have to look.

The place with the fountain is serene and lovely. There are blooming roses everywhere, trees provide pleasant shade, and the sound of the bubbling fountain is soothing. I'm praying it's not a place for a murderer to clean up.

We walk around the base looking for anything out of place, and at first glance it all looks pristine. The pale pink and white water lilies are perfect. I'm ready to heave a sigh of relief—until Olivia says, "What's that under that leaf?"

I look closely, and there is indeed something under the leaf. I find a stick and use it to try to give it a poke, but I can't reach it.

"You're going to have to get in the water," Olivia says.

"Why me? You could, too."

"I can't get these pants wet. They were expensive and need to be dry cleaned."

"Olivia Duncan, we bought those together at Target. They can certainly be washed."

"Okay. I don't want to see what that is so I'm not getting in the water. This all gives me the creeps."

"Fair enough. I don't particularly want to, either, but here goes."

I kick my shoes off and step into the water, trying to push the image of the murderer doing the same thing out of my mind. The water isn't very cold, and it only comes up about five inches on my legs. I wade over to the lily, close my eyes and reach down for whatever is hiding under the leaf. It's a piece of dark blue cloth, possibly from a shirt or jacket. I get out of the water and show it to Olivia.

"This looks like it was torn from a piece of clothing. What do you think?"

She turns it over in her hands. "Does this mean the murderer cleaned himself off in there and then walked away shirtless? That would have made him very noticeable."

"Not necessarily. The killer could've been wearing two layers of clothes. And maybe it isn't from a shirt. The fabric feels like cotton, but it's been in the water for a few days, which may have softened it up."

I pick up my shoes and stick the piece of cloth in my pocket. As we walk across the grass, Olivia says, "Mal was wearing a thin, dark blue jacket the day we arrived. I remember thinking it looked so nice over her white top. You don't suppose…?"

I shake my head. "That can't be. I don't want to even think about it." But I wish I could peek in Mal's closet and see the jacket hanging there.

Chapter 15

"I'm so frustrated. There's absolutely no info about a Vivian Kettani."

Olivia and I are sitting on my bed, each with our laptops open to Google. And drinking coffee, thanks to Suad, who cheerfully made a pot for us.

My good friend agrees. "It would help if we knew her maiden name? Do you know if she's been married before? The only thing I can find is a small article about the Kettanis attending a charity function. It only mentions a Mme. Kettani, not even her first name."

"There's so much to think about. Is the killer a family or staff member or stranger? I'm ruling out stranger because a stranger wouldn't know about the fountain. Is someone really following Mal, or is she imagining it? And what about the papers we found in the hiding place. Was Fatima having Kadem investigated because she thought he was being unfaithful? And if so, was Vivian the other woman? She seems like a poor substitute for his wife, but Fatima was very sick with cancer, and maybe he couldn't cope with it. Or was someone else being investigated?"

Olivia adds more milk to her coffee. "I'll bet Vivian would've had no problem hitching her star to Kadem, who has piles of money. I don't think the fact he was married would bother her at all."

"You're probably right. Kadem is a smart man, though. He doesn't strike me as someone who could be used. If Vivian did marry him for his money, I'm sure he knows it."

"Could this be the reason Mal seems so upset and unhappy?" Olivia asks. "She was so close to Fatima. And Vivian certainly is hostile toward her. Living in this house can't be pleasant for her."

"Have a look at this article I found. I was hunting for more info about Vivian, but this came up. It was in a Moroccan magazine translated into English. It's not about Vivian, but it is about the Kettani Ruby."

Kadem Kettani found the exquisite Kettani Ruby quite by accident when he was a young man working in what was then known as Burma. Strange as it may sound, M. Kettani happened upon a bazaar in a remote village and bought what he thought was a pretty stone. Its value became known years later when he took it to a jeweler to have it made into a ring. The stone is a six carat, pure, vibrant, dark red color known as pigeon blood.

"No wonder Vivian's knickers were in a knot when she found out it was missing," Olivia says. "I can imagine she would've enjoyed owning it. But I wonder where it is and how it disappeared from the safe."

I don't have an answer, so I close my laptop, finish my coffee and slide off the bed. We need to get ready to start the day. We're going to go walking with Mal today to try to trap the guy she says is following her. I'm touching up my makeup in the bathroom when Olivia peers in the door and tells me to hurry. I turn around to greet her, and the little pendant necklace I bought in the souk falls off my neck and lands in the toilet. Fortunately, the toilet is clean. I fish it out, dry it off and stick it in my pocket. The clasp is broken, but there's no time to worry about that now.

"This is making me so nervous." Mal's face is the color of chalk, and her head keeps swiveling right and left.

"Relax. Aziz is behind us, and he'll be on the lookout for the man. If someone has been stalking you, we'll get him."

I sound calm, but I'm not, mostly because I'm once again overthinking. I can't get the thought out of my mind that Mal might've had something to do with the disappearance of the Kettani Ruby, and the person following her thinks so, too. He's hoping to either steal it from her or find out where she's hidden it. My rational self tells me this is ridiculous, but at the moment, my rational self is on vacation.

Olivia knows what I'm thinking and keeps glaring at me as we cross the street to Jemaa el Fna and enter the square. "No one can follow us in here," Mal mutters. "There are too many people."

But she's wrong. I look behind me and see a man fitting the description of her follower wearing a dark hat pulled down over his head and dark glasses. And I don't see Aziz. We weave our way through the throngs of people shopping at the food places in the square. I'm okay staying out here where I can see blue sky, and I'm hoping Mal doesn't intend to enter the crowded, claustrophobic indoor souks. But she heads straight for them.

I'm not a fan of the souks. It was a unique experience once, but that was enough. But once again we're shoulder to shoulder with people, and once again I'm almost overcome with the noise, smells and warm bodies squishing against us. In spite of the crush of people, I manage to glance behind me and see the head with the hat. There are several people between us, and he's not looking directly at us. Coincidence? Is someone really following Mal? To find out for sure, I tell Mal and Olivia to duck into the next shop and see if he passes us. We enter an antique stall and nervously look out, waiting for the man to come by. The proprietor greets us with a smile and an offer of mint tea. When Mal politely tells him we're not interested in buying anything, his smile fades, and he goes back to reading his paper.

"I don't see him," Olivia whispers. "I'm sure he hasn't gone past."

Mal is almost twitching with quivering nerves. "I told you someone was following me. Now do you believe me?"

"I do," I say. "Where is Aziz? Can you give him a call?"

We ignore the shop keeper who's now glaring at us as we wait for Aziz to answer his phone.

"That's odd," Mal says. "He isn't answering, and he always does." Her eyes are huge as she grabs my arm. "What do you suppose has happened to him?"

"I'm sure he's fine," I say as I peel her fingers off my flesh. "Let's get out of here and keep walking. There are three of us and one of him. The odds are totally in our favor." I hear Olivia snort and ignore her.

We leave the stall and try to walk with our arms linked, which is impossible to do in the crowd. Mal breaks away and walks fast, pushing her way past people, and my attempts to call out to her are drowned in the noise. Olivia and I have been clutching each other, but two men smoking evil-smelling cigarettes barge between us. Olivia is pushed to the right, into a stall selling copper pots. I try to follow her, but that's also impossible, and I'm reluctantly swept forward.

I'm beginning to be scared. I feel hands touch my jacket, and I pull away. I long to turn around and find my way back to the entrance, but the crush of people prevents it. Suddenly a strong hand grabs each elbow and forces me forward out of the throng, and for one moment I'm hoping Aziz has found me. But Aziz can't be on both sides of me at once. I try to stop and speak, but the hands pull harder, and soon I'm in a stall that smells of leather and cigarette smoke. Three men with beards and moustaches sit on the floor drinking tea. They barely look up as I'm propelled through the stall and out a back door.

Now a hand is clamped over my mouth, and a low guttural voice says, "You go home. You want to die?" The English is broken, but the threat is unmistakable. I most certainly do not want to die. Another hand grabs my bag and dumps it out on the ground.

A young boy with dark hair and a dirty face passes us, stares briefly and carries on. Powerful hands pull me until we reach a dark corner of the souk, and now I'm terrified something worse is going to happen. But suddenly my captors release my arms, push me to the ground and disappear. When I'm sure they're gone, I sit up and try to control my breathing. My heart is pounding so fast and hard, I'm afraid it's going to give up and stop. As I wobble to my feet, I see the boy is back.

"I take you out. Five dirham."

I've heard all kinds of stories about kids offering to guide gullible tourists through the souks and then robbing them, but I'm in no position to turn down help. I can either try to find my way out by myself or hope this young boy is honest and will lead me to the exit. I choose the latter, praying this kid is only interested in the money I intend to give him and not taking me into more danger.

I'm beyond relieved when I recognize the entrance to the square. The boy holds out his grubby hand, accepts the five dirham and runs back into the souks. My knees are shaking as I pull out my cellphone and call Olivia.

She answers immediately and sounds quite annoyed. "Where

are you? I've been looking all over. And where's Mal?"

"Olivia, please tell me where you are and let's get out of here. I have no idea where Mal is."

"I'm in the café that overlooks the square. I figured I'd wait for you here."

"I'll be at the door." I pause. "Please, Olivia, can we get going."

Her voice changes. "On my way. Hang on."

We find a taxi at the edge of the square, and we don't talk until I'm sure we're on our way back to the house. I finally tell Olivia what happened in the souk and am instantly sorry because she gasps and turns pale.

"We have to get out of here, Julia. Go home. This is nuts. We haven't done anything and don't know anything. And where's Mal? Why isn't she worried about us?"

"I don't know. I'm also wondering about Aziz. Where is he? And I'm wondering who the men were who grabbed me. I've never seen them before—not that I had a chance to have a good look."

We reach the Kettani house, and the taxi proceeds slowly up the long drive. When it stops at the top, I pause before getting out. "I've had it, Olivia. I don't want any more anonymous men trying to scare me to death. They've succeeded. I'm scared. I'm also done. I love Mal and Peter, but they can figure out whatever is going on here. As soon as Dirk and Oliver arrive, I want to leave."

I'm just about to reach for the door when it flies open, and a wild-eyed Mal bursts out.

"Where have you been? I've been looking all over for you. You won't believe what's happened. Come and look for yourself."

I step past her and walk into the spacious hall. “Not here,” she says as she pulls my arm. “Someone broke in and the whole house has been trashed. Look at this.”

The beautiful vases are now broken shards of porcelain. Cushions from the couch have been tossed on the floor. The back of a velvet chair has been slashed.

“It’s even worse in Kadem’s office,” Mal says. She’s actually wringing her hands. “Who would do something like this? And what are they looking for?”

“I don’t know. Have you talked to the staff? Or called Kadem? Or maybe the police?”

“I tried to call Peter, but he’s not answering. I think they’re still on the plane. I asked Suad, and she said no one heard anything.” She looks down at the floor. “I’m not calling the police.”

I don’t understand this. “But why not? Your house has been vandalized.”

She shakes her head. “Kadem doesn’t like the police coming here. He says our staff can take care of any problem.”

“And I’m certain they can.” Vivian strides across the room. “I’ve already asked Brandon to search the grounds for intruders, although I don’t think he’ll find anyone.”

Speaking of the devil, Brandon comes into the room. He looks grim. “I can’t find anything. I have no idea how this person managed to get in here. I suspect someone from the kitchen might have opened the door, but I’ll get that sorted out later.”

“Thank you, Brandon. Mr. Fieldstone arrived shortly after we discovered this, and he didn’t see anything. I’m afraid we may never know who did this.”

Mal’s displeasure is written all over her face. “Why is Corey Fieldstone here? Peter never mentioned seeing him again.”

“Mr. Fieldstone said he had an appointment with Kadem this

afternoon. I had to apologize for my husband, who obviously forgot. In any event, I'm glad he's here. This break-in has made me extremely nervous, and it's good to have strong men to protect us." She looks around the room. "The staff will soon have this cleaned up. It's very troubling to think someone broke those lovely vases. I believe they were from an ancient Chinese dynasty. Priceless. I shall inform the insurance company."

Vivian sails off to attend to her guest, and Mal snickers. "Those vases weren't from an ancient Chinese dynasty. Fatima bought them online when she was in North Carolina and had them shipped to Morocco. She paid $267 for both of them and was delighted with the price. It cost double that to ship them."

"I'm glad to hear they weren't valuable, but Mal, someone was obviously looking for something. Do you have any idea what that could be?" I'd love to ask her why she ditched us in the souks, but now doesn't seem like a good time.

"It looks like the intruder didn't have time to get to the bedroom area, but I'd check your belongings, just to make sure nothing is missing. I'm so sorry about this, Julia. Make sure you do a complete inventory and let me know. You didn't come to Morocco for all this trouble. Again, I'm so sorry."

"Don't worry. I don't have anything valuable in my room. I had my wallet with me, and the only costume jewelry I have is what I'm wearing—two bracelets, a topaz ring Tony gave me and the pendant I bought in the souk. I fixed the clasp on the pendant using my tweezers as pliers."

"I'm relieved to hear that. One more thing. Would you please join us for dinner tonight? I know Vivian has invited Corey Fieldstone, and I need you and Olivia to be there, too. The man annoys me immensely. He's so…"

"In your face? Obnoxious? Social climbing? Have I missed anything?" Olivia asks. "The man makes me itch."

Mal actually laughs. “Well said, Olivia. So will you come to dinner? If we collectively ignore him maybe he’ll take the hint. Every once in a while we learn of people who are dying to know Kadem Kettani and will do almost anything to meet him. I think Corey is one of those people. Harmless but irritating. By the way, Peter hardly remembers him.”

“Sure, we can do that. I share your opinion of Corey, but we can certainly get through one dinner.”

I don’t want to do this, but there’s no way to get out of it.

Chapter 16

This is excellent wine," Corey says. He swirls the liquid around in the glass. "See the legs? That means it's good. I wouldn't bring anything that wasn't."

He is preening like a peacock, and Mal, Olivia and I are thumping each other under the table. It is, however, nice to enjoy a glass of wine. It isn't served in the Kettani house, but since Kadem isn't home, and we're all citizens of other countries, Vivian has deemed it okay.

"It's excellent, Mr. Fieldstone. Thank you for bringing it. I'm afraid we don't have an adequate cellar in this house. M. Kettani doesn't drink alcohol."

"I'm delighted you like it, and please call me Corey, Mme. Kettani. I feel like Nabil and I are almost brothers."

The lady of the house bestows a beatific smile on the obnoxious one. "Very well. And you must call me Vivian."

I nearly choke on my wine. Corey is a simpering idiot, and he must want to be in the Kettani inner circle very badly. He's nowhere close to being Peter's brother. I stab an asparagus spear and say, "Where's your wife, Corey?"

He takes a sip of wine. "She isn't feeling well and opted to stay in the hotel." He turns to Olivia. "I understand your friend from England is arriving soon. Oliver Parker Smythe is certainly a well-known name in upper class circles."

That remark makes me gag, and daggers are flashing out of Olivia's eyes. "How did you learn about him, Corey, or that he's coming here?"

"Oh dear, have I said something wrong? I think Malika told me, or perhaps it was you, Mme. Kettani—I mean Vivian. Why do you ask? Was his visit supposed to be a secret? I'd certainly love to meet him."

Vivian nods. "I intend to have some sort of social gathering when he and…ah…Julia's friend arrive. I thought perhaps some tennis and dinner by the pool."

These are terrible ideas—and where on earth does she intend to play tennis? I know Olivia and I are looking forward to time by ourselves with Oliver and Dirk. I chuckle to myself thinking how Corey would enjoy knowing they were flying here in Oliver's private plane.

"I understand his lordship is arriving in his own plane. How exciting. I'd love to see it. Do you suppose you could arrange that, Malika?"

The man has no shame. And how does he know all this? Olivia and I look accusingly at Mal, who seems to have loose lips. But our friend isn't listening to the conversation. Her eyes are down, and she's pushing a delicious piece of fish around on her plate.

"I'm afraid they won't have time for any social events," I say. "They won't be here long."

Corey isn't ready to take no for an answer. "Surely we'll be able to find a mutually agreeable time…"

When Suad bursts into the dining room, I figure something has gone wrong with the chocolate soufflé, but when she races over to Vivian and unloads a torrent of French, I know I'm wrong. Mal and Olivia, who both understand her words, immediately jump to their feet. Mal knocks her glass of wine over, and it spills onto the floor.

"This is terrible. Enough! Enough!" She sinks down in her chair and buries her head in her hands, and I look to Olivia for a translation.

"Aziz was found unconscious in a souk. He's been taken to the hospital," she says in a low voice. "He was mugged."

"Oh my! That explains why he didn't bring us home today. Is he going to be okay?"

"I think so. They don't have much information."

I glance at Vivian, who seems more annoyed than upset. "This certainly isn't a good time to have something like this happen. Kadem isn't here, and he usually handles situations like this."

"I'll be glad to help any way I can, Vivian." Corey puts a hand on her shoulder. "You shouldn't have to worry about this."

Mal comes to life with a vengeance. She flies to her feet and stops an inch from Corey's face. "Then who should worry about this, Corey? She's the lady of the house, although she hardly knows Aziz. And you don't know him at all. Why are you here?"

"Malika! I think you need to apologize and then go to your room and rest." Vivian's face is purple. "That's no way to talk to a guest."

"Don't tell me what to do, Vivian. And he's your guest, not mine. I repeat, Corey. Why are you here?"

Corey looks amused. "I'm sorry if you find my company offensive. I'm only trying to be helpful."

"That's not what you're trying to do. I have your number, and it's not going to work." She wants to say more but sees Suad tugging at my arm. "What is it now, Suad?"

"She wants us to come with her to the staff quarters," Olivia says. "There's something she wants to show us."

"Very well," says Mal, " have no idea what that could be but go ahead. I'm going to bed."

Darn! I have some questions I really want to ask her. "I wish we could talk for a minute, Mal."

She gives me a hug. "Later, Julia. I'm beat, worried about Aziz, and I have heavy things to do tomorrow. Have a good night."

My questions will have to wait. Right now we have to go with Suad. Corey intends to come with us, but I put out my hand and say, "Stay," so forcefully he stops. "We're good here. Perhaps it's time for you to go back to your hotel."

Vivian is furious, but I don't give her a chance to speak. She's still sputtering when we head out of the dining room.

We reach the staff quarters and find one man with a bloody mouth and the other with a swollen left eye. Olivia translates what they're saying.

"The man with the swollen eye is accusing the other man of trying to steal from Abdul's sister."

"Why would anyone want to…?"

"Shh, I'm trying to hear. Swollen Eye says he was visiting Abdul's sister. They had gone out to get something to eat, and when they returned they found Busted Lip sneaking out of the house. The two men got into a fight, which seems fairly obvious."

We both turn around to see Mal has joined us. "I decided I need to know what's going on in this house." She confronts Busted Lip. "What were you doing at Abdul's house? You had no business going there. You stay away from there. Do you hear me?"

She's screeching in English, so I'm fairly certain Busted Lip doesn't understand her words, but there's no mistaking her anger. This guy is being yelled at by his employer, so you'd think he'd be somewhat subdued, but instead of contrition, he whirls around on Mal. And what he says makes Olivia gasp before she can translate.

"You are the evil one. You and the other. You are the reason Abdul is dead. I spit on you."

Lordy! Can the day get any worse?

As we walk through the staff quarters, I notice one room with the door open and clothes heaped on the small bed. I recognize jeans and a Detroit Tigers jacket in the pile.

"This must be Brandon's room," I say, peering inside. "He's not very neat, is he?"

Before Suad or Olivia can stop me I step into the room and look around. I can understand not finding any personal items in Abdul's room because he's dead, but Brandon isn't, and there's nothing here. There's a bottle of water on the table, plus a toothbrush and toothpaste, and that's all. But what I find in the closet makes me suck in my breath, which must have been audible because Olivia is beside me in a flash.

"What's wrong? What was that sound?"

I point to the closet. "Do you see what I see?"

"Lordy, I do."

It's a dark blue jacket with a ripped pocket.

Olivia pulls me aside and whispers in my ear. "Suad said she has to talk to me. Are you okay waiting here?"

"I'll go to the kitchen." When we passed through I saw delicious-looking, gooey pastry, and I'm hoping it's still there.

It is. I help myself to a piece of delicious *m'hanncha,* a pastry filled with a tasty almond paste and shaped like a snake and make a cup of tea. I eye a second piece but decide I don't need it. And Olivia should be back any minute. Twenty minutes later, she returns, and her face is creased in worry. I offer her a cup of tea and wait until she's settled at the table.

"What did Suad want to talk about?"

Olivia squeezes lemon into her tea and takes an agonizingly long time to answer. "This isn't good, Julia. You know how the staff gossips. The kitchen ladies are convinced Mal is seeing a man when she goes out, and the man isn't her husband. They admire Kadem and Peter. They are hostile to Vivian, but they seem to be afraid of Mal."

"How on earth could they be afraid of Mal? She's such a kind, gentle person. It doesn't make sense."

Olivia sighs heavily. "I hated hearing all this. We know Mal. I don't think there's a mean bone in her body. It's so out of character, but who knows. Incredible as it may sound, maybe we're wrong about her. Remember the day we arrived here and had to wait for Mal because she was supposedly on the phone? She wasn't. Suad told me she came in the kitchen door seconds before she greeted us. The kitchen door, Julia. Was she washing blood off her hands in the fountain after killing Abdul?"

"Have you completely lost your mind? Of course she wasn't." I try desperately to remember what Mal was wearing that day, but I can't. When we get back to Wake Forest I'm going to start taking gingko biloba. My short-term memory definitely needs some attention. "She couldn't possibly have killed Abdul, run to the fountain, washed herself off, returned to the house and calmly greeted us. It's just not possible. And another thing—what reason would she have for killing Abdul?"

Olivia sinks lower in her chair. "I don't know, Julia. Suad thinks it all has to do with the Kettani Ruby. The staff has seen Mal all over the house, looking in empty rooms and opening boxes and things in the storage area. And Mal often leaves the house for a destination that isn't on her calendar. The ladies think she's meeting a man, and Abdul found out and threatened to tell Peter so Mal killed him. One of the men on the staff happened to see her meet a man at a riad. The riad was a low budget bed and breakfast place in the city—not somewhere a Kettani would visit."

"This is absolute rubbish. And why is Suad telling you all this? As I've said before, we're guests here, and we're leaving soon. What can we do?"

"I suppose she's looking for advice. And who should she tell? Should she go to Kadem and say they think his daughter-in-law murdered someone? Or should they tell Vivian? They really don't like her."

By now I've unconsciously devoured two more pieces of pastry. I tell myself that's okay because calories consumed in a foreign country don't actually stick to a body.

"So what I'm thinking is," Olivia says, "we should follow Mal when she goes out tomorrow. Maybe that will give us some answers. I can't believe our good friend killed anyone, and I'd like to prove she didn't."

"That's a good idea, but we don't have a car. I assume someone on the staff will drive her since Aziz can't. I think calling a taxi and sitting in it until Mal leaves might be a bit obvious." An idea occurs to me. "Maybe we could borrow the car Suad drives. I've seen her unload groceries from a little red one."

Olivia jumps to her feet. "I'll ask her." She hurries out of the kitchen and is back before I can finish another piece of pastry. "She says of course. The car belongs to the house, but no one will miss it for a few hours."

Great. Now all we have to do is try to figure out when Mal is leaving and sit in wait for her.

I'm surprised to see Mal doesn't have a driver. As Olivia and I sit in the little red car and wait, Mal drives past us, and she's all by herself in a gray Fiat. Instead of going down the driveway, she turns down a dirt road at the back of the property. I proceed at a safe distance behind her and soon we are on the main road. I'm concentrating so hard on not having a collision, I can't even yell, "Would you look at that? There's another way out of here."

Driving through Marrakech isn't my favorite thing to do. As I told Olivia, just because I managed to do it once doesn't mean I'll be able to do it again. And I certainly won't be able to with my eyes closed. I force myself to open them and look at the cars tearing around. Mal drives fast, and she also has the advantage of knowing where she's going. We weave through heavy traffic, and twice I slam on the brakes to avoid being smacked by an oncoming vehicle. I'm dismayed to see she's heading in the general direction of the souks, a place I never want to visit again.

I follow her onto Avenue Mohammed V, and for a while she's a comfortable two cars in front of me. Then she makes a sudden left turn without using her signal, and I can't turn in time. I take the next left and hope I'll find her somewhere in front of me.

"Look here," Olivia says. "I pulled up a map of Marrakech on my phone, and Mal turned onto a dead-end street. All we have to do is get back there."

That sounds easy, but it's not. Trying to get back there nearly costs me my sanity. Every time I think I'm going in the right direction I end up on a street that takes me in a circle. I pass the Koutoubia mosque three times before I finally, quite by accident, drive down the right road.

Olivia claps her hands. "Excellent! Now all we have to do is look for her car."

I'm sweating so heavily my hands are slipping off the wheel.

If we ever get us out of here, I vow to never attempt driving in Marrakech again. Now I drive up and down the street twice before Olivia yells, "There's her car! Pull over by that tree."

I park a short distance from Mal's car and look around. We're in front of a riad, a Moroccan bed and breakfast. Some are very fancy. This one is not.

"What do you think we should do?" Olivia asks. "Should we sit out here and wait?" She gives me a questioning look because we're both thinking the same thing. What is Mal doing here? Do we honestly want to know? If she's here for the usual reason most people meet at a hotel in the middle of the day, we could be here for hours.

I get out of the car and peer through the iron gate at the front of the property. There's a courtyard with a tired potted palm tree in the middle. Beyond the courtyard are a series of rooms built in a semicircle. The courtyard is empty, and all the doors are closed.

"Do you think she's here?" Olivia shakes her head. "I guess I'm hoping she's not."

I point to a small shop and a café. "Let's go have a look. If she's not having tea or buying something, I guess we can assume she's in one of those rooms."

She's not in either place. The shop is empty and only one person is sitting in the café. "Let's wait in the car for a bit. If she doesn't come out soon we'll leave because we'll have our answer."

Olivia opens her bag and pulls out two bags of chocolate chip cookies and offers me one. "I brought these from home. Might as well eat them now."

I open the bag and take a bite. "Did you ever dream on that Royal Air Maroc flight across the ocean we'd ever be spying on our good friend or that I'd be clonked on the head or we'd find a man murdered on our friend's driveway? I naively assumed we'd do our key lime pies and spend the rest of the time sightseeing."

"Never. Our friends back home wouldn't believe our stories."

I poke Olivia on the arm. "Look. Someone's in the courtyard, and I think it's Mal, and she's not alone. Quick! Duck."

Olivia and I scrunch down in the seat, but I have to see what's going on. I risk being caught and peek over the dashboard in time to see Mal and a man get into her car. The man is what my grandmother called portly, has gray hair and definitely doesn't look Moroccan. Mal backs carefully out of her parking space and heads to the street. I follow, grinding gears as I shift. We've brought disguises, and now Olivia puts on a floppy hat and sunglasses.

With my right hand I reach into the back and pick up the only disguise I could find at the house—a brightly colored shower cap. I tuck my hair into it and add big round, red sunglasses. Olivia bursts out laughing. "You look like you belong in a circus."

"That's okay. I'm good as long as she can't recognize me. Now let me concentrate on following Mal."

Ten minutes later, I park three cars behind her on a side street full of shops. We watch from the car as Mal and the man enter one of them. We can't tell what kind of a shop it is, but there's a sign outside that might help us. The only problem is—it's in Arabic.

Olivia solves the problem by taking a photo with her cell phone. "I have an app that translates foreign languages into English. Let's give it a try—and look at this. The sign says, "Purveyors and Purchasers of Fine Gems and Jewelry. Why do you suppose Mal is in there?" And who's the dude?"

"I don't know who the dude is, but I have a sinking feeling I know why Mal is there. I'll bet it has something to do with the Kettani Ruby. I think we need to have a chat with our friend now."

Chapter 17

"First of all, Olivia and I want you to know we love you like a sister, and that will never change."

I'm so nervous, my knees are knocking like castanets. Mal looks like a deer caught in headlights. Then three of us are sitting at a table by the pool, which is the only place we can talk without being overheard. The late afternoon sun has turned the garden a warm orange, and the air is soft and fragrant, but I'm far too tense to enjoy it.

"Why are you being so serious, Julia? You're actually scaring me." Her face is pale and stressed, certainly not like our happy, chatty friend.

"We don't mean to scare you, but we've learned some things we think we should share with you."

"What things? I can't imagine what you're talking about. You haven't been here long enough to learn anything."

This is starting out badly, and I look at Olivia for help.

"The thing is, Mal, you've been really busy, so you may not be aware of things that have been happening." Olivia is trying to be tactful, but if we proceed this slowly we'll still be here next year."

"Let's begin at the beginning," I say. "For instance—on the day we arrived at your home. You couldn't meet us because you were on the phone. Mal," I say softly, "we know you weren't."

Mal stares at me. "What on earth are you talking about?"

"You know…that was the day Abdul was killed."

Mal gasps so loudly I'm afraid she's going to pass out. "Are you trying to say I had something to do with his death? How could you possibly think that, Julia? I thought you were my friend."

"I am your friend. *We* are your friends. But there have been some confusing things happening. When we found out you hadn't told us the truth about being on the phone, well…"

Mal puts her head down on the table and buries it in her arms. "I can't stand this anymore," I hear her murmur.

I stand up and put my arm around her shoulder. "Please don't be upset, Mal. We're with you 100%. Of course we don't think you had anything to do with Abdul's death." And in this moment I believe my words.

She looks up and tears are cascading down her cheeks. "You don't understand, Julia. It's terrible here, and the awful part is I don't know what to do."

Now Olivia is next to her and we both have our arms around our friend. "Can we help? We're not trying to pry, but we sure are ready to listen."

She gulps twice and wipes her eyes on her sleeve. "It would honestly feel good to talk about it. Peter tries to listen, but I don't think he really hears me because he's so involved in business with Kadem. I'll admit I'm going crazy."

"We're going to need some wine for this," Olivia says.

Mal agrees. "I don't know, though, where you're going to get wine, but let me call the kitchen for some food."

I laugh. "Not necessary. We'll get it."

"I don't understand. How can you get it?"

"Long story, but we have plenty of time to tell it. There will be a short break while I find food and drink for us."

I go to the kitchen, find Suad and organize wine from our private stash, cheese and biscuits. Before long Suad walks across the lawn carrying a tray. She puts it on the table in front of us, grins broadly and leaves.

Mal picks up the bottle of cold white wine. "I don't understand this at all. Where did she get this? We don't have wine in the house. And why was Suad smiling?"

I pour the chilled Chablis into three glasses. "Here's to answers. We need some and so do you."

We explain how we became friendly with Suad when we were making key lime pie in the kitchen and how Suad and the whole staff loved Abdul and want his killer found.

"They talked to us because they didn't feel they could talk to the family, Mal. They don't like Vivian and didn't want to bother Kadem."

I'm skirting around mentioning the knife because Mal already seems shocked, and I have no idea what she'll do if she finds out her cook is hiding the probable murder weapon.

We tell her our theory about where Abdul was killed. This stuns her because the official story from Kadem is Abdul was murdered in the street in a mugging gone wrong. We also tell her about finding fabric in the fountain and broken branches in the garden, which point to a scuffle.

She takes a long sip of wine and says, "So let me get this straight. You think Abdul was killed in the garden. That would mean his assailant came onto our property. Unless…" It seems to take her forever to form her words. "Someone from the house killed him."

I nod. "That seems to be a possibility." Olivia is giving me a hard stare, and I know she wants me to mention the knife, but I can't. "There's more. I'll admit Olivia and I have been poking around for answers." When she raises her eyebrows in surprise, I say, "The attack on me in the Sahara wasn't an accident. I wasn't assaulted by a random desert marauder. The attack was designed to scare me, just like the recent incident in the souk."

"What incident? I don't know what you're talking about." Mal drains her wine and holds out her glass for more.

"I was going to tell you, but when we arrived home, you all were concerned about the break-in, and I wasn't hurt so we didn't mention it."

By now the sun is down behind the trees, and the outside lights have come on. Suad comes out with another bottle of wine, silently puts it on the table and takes the empty one with her. Mal shakes her head. "I truly don't understand any of this. I feel like I'm visiting another dimension."

"Well, you're not. Now it's your turn. Can you tell us what's wrong?"

Our friend looks genuinely upset. "I promised Fatima I'd keep her secret, but maybe it's time to get help."

"We really don't want to interfere, Mal. If you don't feel comfortable telling us, we understand," I tell her.

"No, we need to get this sorted out." She takes a deep breath and begins. "As I told you before, Fatima and I were good friends. Even before she became my mother-in-law, she and I were close, and as my mother-in-law and mother of my beloved Peter, we became even closer. She suspected Kadem was being unfaithful, even before she was diagnosed with cancer. She told me when he traveled he was occasionally with women who meant nothing to him. That sounds awful, but that's what it was."

"How did she know this?" I interrupt.

"She hired a private investigator and had him followed. She said he never saw the same woman more than once, and the meetings were never in Marrakech. Mostly in Casablanca. Anyway," she continues, "Fatima didn't like this, but since it didn't seem to affect her marriage, she chose to ignore it. That is —until he met Vivian."

Suad comes out and speaks to Mal in French. After a few minutes, she nods, smiles and goes back in the house.

"Vivian wants to know if we're coming in for cocktails and dinner. Suad is telling her the three of us are having a private moment and will be eating out here. Is that okay?"

"It sure is. Carry on, Mal."

"Vivian was not like the other women. Kadem met her at some charity function in London. I don't think he would have given her another thought, but Vivian had other ideas. Even though she knew he was married, she pursued him relentlessly. The private investigator told Fatima all about Vivian and her obvious intentions. Then Fatima was diagnosed with cancer and had to have chemo and radiation."

Here she pauses. "Now I have to explain about Abdul. He was Fatima's driver since the day she married Kadem and moved here. Fatima had to have someone to talk to about Kadem and Vivian, so Abdul slowly became her confidante. He listened and drove her to all her doctor's appointments. He would have done anything for her.

Now comes the reason I've been so upset and nervous. Fatima knew Vivian was a gold digger, but she worried Vivian was after her husband for more than his bank account. Her goal was acquiring the Kettani Ruby. Before she died, Fatima told me she was going to take the ruby ring out of the safe and give it to Abdul. Abdul was to keep it safe and give it to Peter at a later date. I know this sounds irresponsible on Fatima's part, but you have to understand she trusted Abdul with her life. And the feeling was mutual. He would never betray her."

"Oh my. This is terrible." The words explode out of my mouth.

"Exactly," she says. "Now perhaps you understand why I'm so scattered. The ring is missing. Fatima must have taken it out of the safe. Did she give it to Abdul? The thing that scares me the most—someone else must know all this, and I can't understand how that could happen. If Abdul did have the ring, where is it now? Is this the reason he was killed? Did he have it with him when he was stabbed? And now you tell me someone has been trying to hurt you. Is it because you've been poking around?

We stop talking as Suad brings out a lovely tajine of lamb and vegetables. And bread. "And no garlic," she says with a grin.

"I can't get over Suad," Mal says as she puts a piece of lamb on her plate. "She's marvelous. I guess I never really talked to her."

"She's a wonderful ally for you, Mal," Olivia says. "She knows everything that happens in the house, and she doesn't have a high opinion of Vivian."

We eat in silence, and when Mal pushes her plate away, she continues, "Do you suppose Abdul told someone on the staff about the ring, and now that person has it? I can't imagine he would be that indiscreet, but maybe he was. And I don't think Vivian has it—yet. She terrorized the staff after she and Kadem discovered it was missing. I have to find it," she says earnestly. "I've turned the house upside down looking for it. I even went to a jewelry store yesterday to ask if someone had tried to sell it. My private investigator from Casablanca went with me."

Olivia and I exchange surreptitious glances. So that's what she was doing yesterday when we followed her. We sit and talk until the air becomes too cool to sit outside. “I feel much better,” Mal says as we walk into the house. “And by the way, that day you arrived, and I couldn’t meet you? Peter and I were in the pool house having a…I believe it’s called a nooner.” She grins. “There’s no privacy in this house. I’m so glad we talked. All this has been a terrible weight on my heart.”

I have a weight on my heart, too. Olivia and I left some crucial details out of our conversation. We didn’t mention the knife, where it was found or its present whereabouts. Why didn’t we? I don’t know. Mal is telling the truth. Isn’t she?

Chapter 18

It's barely dawn when my bedroom door opens, and Mal tiptoes in. I smell coffee before I actually see her, but I can feel her standing over me.

"Are you awake?"

I open one eye. "I am now. What's up?"

I can't figure out why my head hurts until I remember the amount of wine the three of us drank last night. I fell asleep before I could process everything Mal told us.

"This is exciting," she says sitting down on the bed. "Drink this coffee. I need you to be alert. I have no idea how this happened or who delivered the message, but someone knows where the Kettani Ruby is. We have to go to Ouarzazate right away." She jumps off the bed and pulls the duvet off me. "Get up. The note says we have to be there by noon, and it's about a three and a half hour drive."

Olivia comes into the room rubbing her eyes. "Why all the noise? I need to sleep."

I try to retrieve the duvet and snuggle under it. "Mal says we have to go somewhere to get info about the ruby." I yawn. "Is there anymore coffee?"

Mal thrusts a piece of paper into my hand. "Have a look at this. Someone delivered it this morning."

I hand the note back to her. "It's in French."

"Sorry. I forgot. It says a Monsieur Paul Moreau will be in Ouarzazate today having lunch by the pool and will have information about the Kettani Ruby. It also says M. Moreau is a sketchy high-end jewelry merchant who sometimes deals in merchandise that may or may not have been acquired honestly. If that's true, he probably wouldn't be willing to talk to me, so it would be good if someone else goes with me."

"How would he know you?" I ask.

"My picture has been in several articles about the Kettani family. I suppose he could recognize me from those."

"I see. It also doesn't say where to meet him. Are you supposed to wander around the town calling his name?"

"Please, Julia. I know this sounds weird, but I have to go. This is the first concrete clue we've had, and I think I know where he'll be. The Riad de Soleil. It's a lovely place, very popular with foreigners. If the ring has fallen into the wrong hands, I'll do anything to get it back."

"Where is this Ouarzazate? I don't understand why we have to go there to get answers."

"Ouarzazate is an oasis at the edge of the Sahara. There's an old Kasbah and great scenery. Several movies have been made there. It's not far from your…ah…desert adventure. Can we please get going now? Maybe this person is actually trying to sell the ring."

"Wait a minute, Mal. If this person has the ring, are we going to try to buy it back? I think my check might bounce."

She scowls. "You're not going to take the wind out of my

sails. Maybe the person simply has info about it. I'd welcome that, too. And please don't keep giving me reasons why this doesn't make sense. I know it doesn't, but I have to at least find out what he knows. What if he actually does have the ruby? I have to find out, and for that I need you and Olivia.

I'm not trying to burst her happiness bubble. I'm just trying to make her think. And I'm also longing to go back to sleep.

She strides to door and turns around to glare at me. "I'm not going to miss a chance to find the ring. Are you coming with me? I hope so. I don't want to go alone."

I crawl out of bed and hunt for some clothes. Of course, we're going with her. I have no idea who this M. Moreau is, but considering everything that's happened so far, Olivia and I aren't going to let her walk into possible danger by herself. It makes perfect sense to have the three of us walk into it together. Lordy!

One hour later we're in a silver Mercedes whizzing down the road with Mal at the wheel.

"I simply took Peter's car," she laughs. "I think mine was being serviced. Peter's driver was upset, but there was nothing he could do. I also had a bit of a confrontation with Vivian, who seems to think she also controls the vehicles. She wanted to know where I was going and why I was taking the car, and I told her it wasn't any of her business. I guess now it's open warfare." I notice her knuckles are white as she clenches the steering wheel. "She probably shouldn't have told me I shouldn't take the car. I hate the way she's taking over the house, and there doesn't seem to be anyone to stop her. Kadem has no idea what's going on because he's away so often on business.

"Anyway," she continues, "can you imagine how great it would be to find the Kettani Ruby? The police have questioned everyone in the house, and Kadem has offered a substantial reward for information leading to the recovery but so far, nothing."

"Let's suppose you're able to find it. Shouldn't you give it to Kadem rather than Peter? After all, he did buy it, and Fatima was his wife."

She jerks her head to look at me. "Are you nuts? Fatima would hate that. No, if I'm lucky enough to find it, I'm following one of his mother's last wishes and giving it to her son."

As we talk, I'm trying to ignore how fast Mal is driving. These are the same terrifying curves I recently navigated, but at least there's no car behind us trying to push us off the road. Still, I'm hoping to reach our destination in one piece. I glance at Olivia to see if she's as nervous as I am, but her sunglasses are covering her eyes so it's hard to tell.

"By the way," Mal says. "I found out where M. Moreau is staying and made reservations for us at the same place. I was right. It's the Riad de Soleil. I just have to figure out how to keep him from seeing me."

"Do you also have a plan?" I ask. "How are we going to approach this man?"

She drums the steering wheel with her fingers. "I have a few ideas. They sort of involve you."

Oh my! "Let's hear them."

"I was thinking we could contact him and say we're calling for a wealthy American who wants to buy fabulous, unusual jewelry." She gives me a sideways glance. "That would be you. We can dress you up a bit, fix your hair, use some makeup and make you look expensive. Olivia could be your personal assistant. No offense, Olivia, but Julia can be slightly arrogant, and you don't have an arrogant bone in your body."

"I'm certainly not arrogant," I protest. "I just don't like people to argue with me when they're for the most part wrong."

Mal winks at Olivia in the rearview mirror. “See what I mean?”

I think this plan needs some work. “What if he asks how we heard about him?”

“I googled his name, and he actually does have a reputation as a jewelry merchant,” Mal replies. “It appears he also has a legitimate business. We can say we saw an article about him in a magazine, and through luck we happened to be at the same hotel. Ouarzazate is a tourist destination. That won’t sound strange.”

The whole thing sounds strange to me, but I’ll do anything to help Mal.

Our hotel in Ouarzazate is gorgeous. The courtyard leading to the rooms has a mosaic tile floor, palm trees and flowers everywhere. The rooms are nice, but what makes the place special is the area around the pool. There are huge pots of blooming cabbage roses and white tables with crisp white cloths. We arrived in time for the buffet lunch set up outside. My mouth waters at the thought of eating the beautiful spread of fresh peppers, tomatoes, carrots, zucchini, watermelon and oranges.

Olivia can read my mind. “Don’t eat anything you can’t peel. I can see you eyeing the tomatoes.”

“Surely it’s safe to eat the vegetables here,” I say, selecting a plump tomato and pepper. “I’ll be fine.”

Mal comes across the pool deck wearing a big smile. “He’s here. I asked at the desk. Now all we have to do is implement our plan.” She frowns at the plate in my hand. “Don’t eat that, Julia. I know it looks appetizing, but you’ll be sorry if you do. Try something from the hot buffet.”

Reluctantly, I ditch my plate and sit down at a table with Mal and Olivia. First things first. We fill our plates with chicken, carrots and onions from the tagine and several pieces of delicious bread. When Mal pushes her empty plate away and pulls out her laptop, we get down to business.

"The lady at the desk told me M. Moreau usually spends time by the pool in the late afternoon. This is a photo of him I found on the internet. Take a good look because we have to be able to identify him."

Olivia and I study the picture of a balding, portly man in his sixties with a large head, beady eyes, a crooked nose and a scar on his right cheek. For some reason he reminds me of a whale—a beat up whale.

"He should be easy to spot," I say. "And here's a question. Suppose he and I are able to achieve some kind of rapport. If he does have the ring, I'm sure he won't whip it out at our first meeting. How is M. Moreau supposed to contact us? If he calls my cell and hears, 'My puppies and I can't take your call right now,' he might get suspicious."

Mal nods. "Good question. We'll use a burner phone. He won't be able to trace that. We need to get you fixed up now, Julia, and rehearse your story. We can't mess this up."

A burner phone? She says it so matter of factly, as if we all use burner phones when we want to hide our identities.

We spend the next two hours in my room. Mal and Olivia take forever choosing the right clothes for me and finally settle on black pants, a crisp white shirt, a maroon jacket and black heels so high I'm afraid of falling.

"Don't try to close the jacket," Mal warns. "It's a bit too small for you. And don't move your arms around too much. The sleeves are pretty tight. And give me that thing you're wearing around your neck. That definitely looks like junk." She takes the pendant I bought in the souk and sticks it in her bag.

Satisfied with my clothes, they move on to my head. It takes two of them to subdue my wild hair, which they slick back, force into a bun and hold in place with almost a whole can of hair spray, and a diamond clip. On one side they allow tendrils to fall over the side of my head to hide my healing wound. I sit still while Olivia concentrates on my face. I'm speechless at the amount of brushes and tubes she pulls out of her bag, because my normal beauty routine consists of eyebrow color, concealer, blush and lip gloss. When she's done, I don't recognize myself. For the ultimate finishing touch, Mal puts a gold bracelet on my wrist and a diamond ring—big enough to choke someone—on my finger.

She steps back to admire her work. "You look amazing and very expensive. Be sure to remember to casually put your hand on the table so he can see your ring. Kadem gave it to me as a welcome to the family gift, and I've never worn it. It's far too ostentatious for me but should catch M. Moreau's attention. If he asks if you want to sell it, say possibly."

"Really? You don't want this anymore, Mal?"

"Let's just say I'd be curious to hear what someone would pay for it. And why not? It means absolutely nothing to me. Now wait here a minute. I have to find a suitable purse for you. You can't take that old thing you carry."

As soon as she leaves the room, I turn to Olivia. "So what do you think? Has she been telling us the truth, or is she somehow involved in the disappearance of the ruby, and we're her totally in the dark, willing stooges."

Olivia smooths an errant hair on my head. "I think she's telling us the truth—but she obviously needs money. I really want to believe her."

"So do I, Olivia. So do I."

Chapter 19

At 4:00 the three of us are lurking behind a palm tree trying to look inconspicuous. We're watching for Monsieur Moreau, and I'm a nervous wreck. I can feel myself sweating, which doesn't bode well for Mal's pretty jacket. I tell myself to calm down and pretend this is a play, and I'm merely a character in it. All I have to do is play a part. This makes me remember when I was in grade school and tried out for the Christmas pageant. I landed the part of a sheep.

We wait for an hour. I've moved from nervous to tired, and the fancy shoes are killing my feet.

Finally we see a bald, stocky man walk out of the hotel and sit down at a table by the pool.

"Do you think that's our guy?" Mal whispers. "He's wearing sunglasses so it's hard to tell."

We send Olivia over to make a positive ID. She saunters past him and gives us the thumbs up behind her back.

"Okay, Julia," Mal says. "It's go time. We'll be at a table next to you and we'll try to hear what he's saying. I'm afraid he might recognize me, so I'll sit with my back to you." She gives me a thump on the back. "Go get him."

I teeter over to him, hoping I look like an American woman with money to burn. I hear Olivia hiss, "Stand up straight. Stop looking at your feet."

He's studying his cell phone, but he has to hear me coming because my heels are clacking across the pool deck. I stop in front of him and say, "May I speak to you for a minute, M. Moreau?"

He looks up and gives me the once over behind his sunglasses. I try to stand still and look expensive.

"Excuse me, madam. Do I know you?"

"You do not, but I'm hoping you will in the future."

"Interesting."

He removes his sunglasses. The photo we saw online was kind to him. In real life his eyes are tiny and too close together, the scar is a vivid slash on his cheek and his belly is so significant it touches the edge of the table. He does make me think of a whale.

"With whom do I have the pleasure?" His English is heavily accented but good.

My name? We'd rehearsed everything but totally forgot to think up a name. I say the first thing that comes into my head. "My name is Stephanie Orca…" I see Olivia slap her forehead and quickly add, "Wesley." Why on earth did I say orca? My subconscious has to stay quiet.

He seems amused. "Why do you want to talk to me, Ms. Wesley?" He points to a chair across from him, indicating I should sit down. "You are an American. Yes?"

"Yes, I am." This is an easy question, but I'm still so tense I can't unclench my fists under the table. I glance at Olivia, who's giving me the "let's move along" sign. "I understand I may be able to purchase some jewelry from you. I'm looking for something very particular."

He leans back in his chair and studies me. "I'm sorry to disappoint you, madam, but I'm simply here for a few days of relaxation. I'm not here to do business."

Now what do I do? I can't stand up and walk away. "M. Moreau, I understand you're a very reputable jeweler in France. I've read articles about you. I know you deal in fine, hard to get pieces. I'm hoping you can help me."

He is quiet for so long I'm afraid he has either fallen asleep or has died. "My jewelry is not for everyone. It is very costly."

"That's fine. Money won't be a problem." I casually stretch out my hand on the table. He's very good at being subtle, but I see him quickly lower his eyes to glance at the ring.

"What kind of jewelry interests you?"

"I like the unusual. Unique. One of a kind things." Olivia smiles and nods at me so I keep going. "For instance, rubies. Big rubies. I hope that doesn't sound vulgar." I'm beginning to amuse myself. I never talk this way.

His porcine eyes narrow. "That would be quite expensive."

I shrug and try to look bored. "Whatever. Do you have anything?"

"I might but certainly not here. I do not carry such things around in my pocket. If you come to my room, I'll be happy to show you some pieces."

Both Mal and Olivia are shaking their heads, but I say, "I'm not able to do that this evening, and I'd like to bring my associate with me. She has a good eye. Would sometime tomorrow be acceptable?"

If he's inviting me to his room for other reasons, it won't be, but he says, "That would be acceptable. Shall we say 10:00?"

I hope he doesn't see my sigh of relief. He doesn't want me for my body.

We hadn't planned to spend the night, but we all agree we can't miss this opportunity to see what M. Moreau has. We have to scramble in the morning to find something for me to wear. I end up putting on the same pants and a sleeveless silk lavender top Olivia wore yesterday. Mal hands a heavy gold rope around my neck, gives my face a once over, and we're off.

Olivia is not happy. As my "associate" she's wearing no makeup, a sweater we found in the trunk of the car and my tennis shoes. "I still don't understand why you think an associate has to look like a bag lady. I don't feel like myself."

"You're supposed to be the sensible one. The one who handles all the money and keeps me from foolish impulse buying."

"I want to firmly state you owe me big time. And I'm pretty sure there are attractive associates."

I pat her hand. "Don't worry. We know you're gorgeous. Let's just do this and get it over with."

As we walk to M. Moreau's room, we invent a name for Olivia. "So you are Salma Johnson, born in Egypt, now an American citizen and married to Sam Johnson. You are also a financial whiz."

"This makes me nervous. I have trouble balancing my own checkbook, so I hope he doesn't ask me any fiduciary questions."

"Listen to you. You even sound smart." We reach the door before she can retort.

M. Moreau greets us warmly and ushers us into his room. "Bonjour, Madam Wesley. Would you care for coffee? Or perhaps your associate?"

I shake my head. "No, thank you. Let's get down to business. I'd like to see what you have."

"I appreciate your directness." He leads us to a table holding an impressive display of jewelry. I see beautiful things but no large ruby ring.

He waves his hand over the table. "Of course, I do not travel with my entire collection of jewelry, but these are items a client asked me to bring to Morocco. They are all one of a kind pieces. Do you see anything you like?"

I frown. "I was hoping to see rubies. Perhaps an important ruby ring?" I give him what I hope is a significant look."

He looks down at his hands and then back at me. "I wouldn't know where to obtain such a ring."

"That's too bad, monsieur. I was hoping you did."

"If the ruby is almost flawless, the ring would surely not be for sale."

"Perhaps not. The ruby I'm imagining is mounted in platinum and surrounded by diamonds."

"I see. Have you seen this ring?"

"No, I haven't, but I'm imagining it exists."

"And if it does exist, madam? And if I were possibly able to somehow find it?"

I almost suck in my breath and then remember I'm supposed to be trying to buy stolen jewelry. "Well, then M. Moreau, you and I would be able to make a deal."

He almost smiles. "You do understand such a fantastic piece would be extremely expensive."

"And as I told you, I don't worry about money."

His voice suddenly becomes hard. "I should tell you I have done an online search for you, and there's no such person as Stephanie Orca Wesley. Who are you?"

I'm ready for this. "Did you honestly think I'd give you my real name. That would be very foolish. Let me assure you, though, the money is real." I turn to Olivia. "Salma, I think we should leave now."

"Wait. I may possibly be able to help you. Not today, but soon. In the meantime, do you see anything that amuses you on the table. There are some pretty little trinkets."

The pendant I bought in the souk is a trinket. The jewelry on this table is exquisite. There are diamond clips and gold bracelets and a particularly gorgeous twisted rope necklace. And a unique ivory elephant pin with an emerald eye and a small ruby garland around its neck. My heart starts pounding because I've seen that pin or one just like it before. Mal often wore it on a green turtle neck sweater and told me it was a gift from Fatima, her mother-in-law. She also showed me the small M engraved on the back. I casually pick it up and turn it over in my hand. The M is tiny, but it's there.

"This is lovely. Is there a story behind it?"

He shrugs. "It's an heirloom piece.

"And the price?"

"The seller wants $50,000. That would be US dollars."

"The seller? This doesn't belong to you?"

"I'm merely the middle man, madam. If you're interested, I suggest you purchase it quickly. There are others interested."

I put the pin back on the table. Somehow I have to take a photo of this so I can show Mal. I hold out my hand and say to M. Moreau, "I might be interested in selling this ring. Would you be able to tell me its value?"

He looks puzzled. "You want to sell this beautiful piece? Do you need money?"

"No, monsieur, I do not need money. My mother-in-law gave me this ring when I was still married to her son. I didn't particularly like either one of them, and I don't want this ring to remind me."

He smiles. "I understand. "If you would hand it to me, I will examine it."

I take it off my finger and give it to him. As he walks to a desk to find his jeweler's loupe, I pull my phone out of my pocket and quickly snap a few photos of the pin and other jewelry and wait for him to finish, which is taking a long time.

When he finally walks over to me, his face is flushed. "This is an exceedingly rare diamond. Your mother-in-law must have at one time liked you very much. It is flawless. I am speechless you want to sell it. It would probably fetch in the neighborhood of $200,000, US, of course. Do you want to leave it here with me? I am sure it will sell quickly."

"Not at the moment, M. Moreau. It would probably be prudent to have another estimate."

"If the price isn't satisfactory, I can attempt to sell it for more."

Just as I thought, but you can't blame the man for trying. I put the ring back on my finger and walk to the door.

"We'll be in touch. If you locate a ruby ring similar to the one I'm seeking, be sure to call me. And I will let you know about selling this one."

He doesn't look happy, but we hurry out. I can't wait to talk to Mal.

Chapter 20

"What! That price is absolutely ridiculous. The pin you saw is costume jewelry. Fatima had a copy made for me after I admired hers, which by the way, is real ivory and jewels. Mine is worth about $200, and I have no idea how this M. Moreau happens to have it."

Olivia, Mal, and I are in the car on our way back to Marrakech, and Mal is understandably upset at the news about her pin.

"And I know the pin in the photo is the copy because of the M on the back. Fatima had it put there so there could be no confusion. What kind of a jeweler is this M. Moreau if he can't tell real from fake."

"How would someone get your pin?" I ask. "Did you know it was missing?"

Mal runs her hand through her hair, which makes me nervous. Two hands on the wheel on this road. "I knew someone had been in my room, but I thought it might have been one of the staff. I never noticed anything missing, but I found a hiding place for things I didn't want anyone to see."

That would be the hole in the floor in the old master bedroom.

"M. Moreau said the elephant piece was on consignment," I say. "That means someone gave it to him to sell, and that person has to be someone in the house."

Mal puts her turn signal on and zooms around a dilapidated truck with a donkey in the back. "Most of the people on the staff have been there forever and are very loyal to the Kettani family. I blame Vivian for this. I told you she's taken things out of the old master bedroom. Who knows what she's sold. Maybe she was the one prowling around in my room."

"There's one more thing," I tell her. "M. Moreau definitely hinted that he had information about the Kettani Ruby. He didn't actually come out and name it, but I know that's what he was talking about. Oh, and he would love to sell your ring for around $200,000."

Mal laughs. "Would he, now. The man is a crook. The ring is worth much more than that." She pauses. "You know what's bothering me here? What if Vivian is selling Fatima's jewelry? I don't think Kadem would like that, but I'd also bet he wouldn't know. Personally, I think Peter should get the jewelry if Kadem doesn't want it."

"But Vivian is Kadem's wife now. Maybe he'd want her to have it."

"I think not, Julia." Mal's voice is crisp. "That simply isn't right."

Rather than argue with her, we drive the rest of the way in silence.

Mal bangs the front door open and charges into the house, and it's obvious she's still sizzling. I'm hoping Olivia and I can divert her from a confrontation until she cools down. As we walk down the hall, we hear voices coming from Vivian's sitting room. Mal puts her hand out like a traffic cop.

"Do you hear that? That sounds like Corey Fieldstone. What would he be doing here? Honestly, that man is so annoying. He knows Peter isn't here."

She stops at the entrance and sticks her head in the door. Vivian and Corey are looking at Vivian's laptop and both are startled to see us. I can feel Vivian staring at me, which is totally understandable since I'm still wearing my Stephanie Orca Wesley face. I tried to brush the gallons of spray out of my hair but only succeeded in creating a stiff bird's nest on my head.

Mal plunges right in. "Hello, Vivian. I see you have a guest."

Vivian doesn't look happy to see us. "I was given to understand you'd be away until this evening."

"Who would tell you that? No one knew where we were going or when we planned to return."

"I wish you wouldn't use that tone, Malika. You sound so combative. I'm quite sure Kadem wouldn't like it."

I see color flood Mal's face and pray Vivian is smart enough to stop talking.

"What tone would that be? And what are you doing here again, Corey? You know Peter isn't here, so you can't use that excuse."

Vivian looks like she wants to kill Mal. "It turns out Corey is quite good at computers, and he's helping me with something."

"What would that be, Vivian? How to sell stuff that doesn't belong to you?"

Oh, Lordy! I suddenly fake a coughing fit which stops conversation for the moment.

"Your friend sounds quite ill, Malika. Perhaps you should take her to her room." Vivian is standing now, and there's no mistaking her anger.

"I'm fine," I croak, although I may have accidentally coughed up a lung. "You all carry on."

Corey pretends to be solicitous. "You don't sound very good, Julia. You should have that cough checked out."

"Thanks for your concern, but I'm good. I think we should go now, Mal," I say as Olivia and I pull her away. I know she wants to say more, but not here. Not now. Mal is shaking as she walks between us to my room.

"That woman makes me so mad. I can't understand how Kadem could marry her."

It would be useless to tell her she may be a tiny bit biased because she loved Fatima. In fact, it would be useless to try to tell her anything right now. Olivia and I get her to my room and decide some food would help. We missed breakfast and now we're starving. I call Suad and soon we have a lovely meal of eggs, bread, tomatoes, grilled vegetables and coffee. It will be easier to deal with Vivian on a full stomach.

Chapter 21

Mal seems to prefer early morning visits. At exactly 6:00 a.m. again this morning, she barges in, comes to my bed and wastes no time making sure I'm awake.

"He wants to meet, Julia. Today. He called on the burner phone and said he had information about the Kettani ring, and he also wants to buy my diamond. You have to meet him again."

"Mal," I say firmly, "Olivia and I are moving our stuff to La Mamounia because, as you know, Dirk and Oliver land soon. So today is impossible."

"Please don't say that, Julia. You're the only one who can meet him."

"Can't do it, so don't ask me again. You know how long I've waited to seem Dirk. I can't stand him up on the day he arrives."

"I'm absolutely begging you. If you can't meet with him, I'll never be able to find the ring or learn what happened to Fatima's jewelry."

Oh dear. She doesn't even try to wipe away the tears that are streaming down her face, and in that moment my heart goes out to her. I want to believe everything she's told us, and I want to forget unanswered questions—such as why she has a burner phone.

When I don't reply she says, "I understand, Julia. I know how much you're looking forward to seeing Dirk."

She's almost to the door when I say, "Wait a minute. If M. Moreau can meet me at La Mamounia later this afternoon, I'll talk to him for a few minutes."

She flies across the room and falls on top of me. "Thank you, thank you, thank you! Now get up. We have to get you dressed."

Olivia thinks I'm crazy, but an hour later I'm wearing gray pants and a snazzy pink silk top. It takes three shampoos to get the gunk out of my hair so we can start over, but I like the end effect. I look like someone who winters in Palm Springs and summers on a yacht somewhere. I hope once again it fools M. Moreau.

"Before I forget, please give me back my pendant," I say to Mal. "You stuck it in your tote yesterday, and I don't have any other jewelry."

She rummages in her bag, pulls out my trinket and tosses it to me. "But don't wear it when you're Stephanie Orca Wesley. She would never put that thing around her neck."

Mal insists we allow her to send us to the airport and hotel in one of their Mercedes. "It's the least I can do, Julia," she says as we get ready to leave. "I've asked M. Moreau to bring the elephant pin with him so you can have a better look. Make sure you see the M. The real one has a small red heart on the foot. And if you can, please try to call me after you meet with him." She smiles. "I know you'll be busy, but please try to find a minute."

Before we leave, Mal asks us to go with her to visit Aziz, who's still recuperating. This is fine with me because I'd like to say goodbye to Suad, so I tell Mal we'll meet her in the kitchen in a few minutes.

Suad sees us coming, wipes her hands on her apron and smiles. "You want food?" She winks. "Maybe wine?" When Olivia explains we're going to the hotel, Suad looks genuinely upset. She takes my hand and says, "You good." She turns to Olivia, and once again I have to wait while they chat.

"She wants to know if we have any news about Abdul. And she's worried about hiding the knife."

I don't know what to tell her. Suad is a nice person caught in a bad situation, and I hate to leave her here. I absolutely have to tell Mal about the knife.

"Tell her not to worry. We'll be back with some answers, and we'll keep in touch." I find a piece of paper in my bag and write down my and Olivia's phone numbers. "Tell her she can call at any time." Although if she tries to talk to me we may have a bit of difficulty understanding each other. As soon as Mal comes into the kitchen, Suad gives me a hug. I hug her back, wishing I could do more.

We find Aziz resting in his bed. He has a bandage around his head and bruises on his face but smiles when he sees Mal. "You are okay?"

"I'm fine," she assures him. "Do you feel like talking?"

He nods. "Bad things are happening."

Mal pulls a chair next to his bed and sits down. "Do you have any idea why someone attacked you?"

He looks at Olivia and me and then back to Mal.

"It's okay, Aziz. You can talk in front of them. They're trying to help me. What can you say?"

He touches his head and winces. "It wasn't a robbery. They searched my body and my jacket, but they didn't take my money. One of the men got very angry when he couldn't find anything. That's when he hit me."

"I'm so sorry," Mal says. "Do you have any idea what they were looking for?"

"Madam Kettani, they were looking for the Kettani Ruby. That's all people talk about in the souks. The famous Kettani Ruby has been stolen from the Kettani family and everyone wants to find it. But no one knows where it is. There are many rumors. One man says someone tried to sell it but couldn't because it is too well-known. Another says it is already out of the country. A third says it is still here in Marrakech at a location outside the city. Several think this is true because the man rumored to have news about the ring isn't one of us. He is a newcomer."

I'm listening to this, but it all sounds like gossip to me. "If people suspect they know who has the ring, why haven't others tried to steal it back?" I ask.

"Who knows what is true, madam? There is always talk. People like to puff their chests out with importance and pretend they have knowledge when they really do not." He hesitates. "This new man. He has only been around here three or four months. He is telling others he knows where the ring is. And it is said he has protection."

"What does that mean? What kind of protection? Spiritual or someone with a gun?" This sounds a bit bizarre. We're not dealing with the mafia.

He shrugs his shoulders. "Just protection. It is said no one should touch him."

Mal jumps to her feet. "Do you know his name, Aziz? And where we can find him?"

Aziz looks at her in alarm. "No, madam. Please do not think of approaching him. People say he is not friendly."

"Let us worry about that. I promise you I'll be careful. So, what is his name, and where can we find him?"

"His name is Jamal," Aziz says reluctantly. "And he is rumored to live in the little village outside Marrakech. It is the one with all the goats and the house with one window."

I roll my eyes at his directions, but Mal claps her hands excitedly. "I know exactly where that is. Thank you so much, Aziz. Take as much time as you need to feel better and be sure to tell Suad if you need anything." To me she says, "Let's hustle," and walks briskly to the door.

Once we're in the kitchen, I stop walking. "I don't know what you're planning, Mal, but have you forgotten Dirk and Oliver arrive today. We're almost on our way to the airport to meet them."

"But, Julia…"

"Mal," I say earnestly, "I have to meet Dirk. No, let me change that. I can't wait to meet Dirk. It's all I've been thinking about. Can't you find someone else to go with you?"

"And who would that be, Julia? Who can I talk to about all this"?

She has a point. Peter isn't here, and she can't talk to Vivian. "Okay," I say reluctantly. "Let me meet Dirk and get settled in the hotel. We don't even know if this mystery man is actually in the village. There's no point hunting for him if he isn't there. We'll figure something out for later."

Her face brightens. "Promise"?

"I'll try my best." And I'm sure Dirk will think I've lost my mind, but I don't say that to Mal.

In the car, I can feel Olivia looking at me. "I can't wait to hear what Dirk says when he sees you. That is, if he recognizes you. He may not."

"Nonsense." I pat my hair. "I'm just cleaned up a bit."

Olivia snorts. "You look completely different."

At the moment, I can't worry about my looks because I'm so excited about seeing Dirk. I never thought another man would make my heart thump like this in anticipation of seeing him. Sometimes I daydream about what I'd say if he asked me to marry him. I swore I'd never do that again, but who knows. He's a successful lawyer in Sacramento, so he probably wouldn't want to move, and I am…well…I love living in Wake Forest, and I do love our little lunchroom so I'm not quite sure how that would work out. And Olivia never expected to meet the love of her life at a small restaurant convention on Hilton Head Island. Technically, she didn't. Oliver Parker Smythe docked his beautiful ocean-going boat in Calibogue Sound at the mouth of the Harbour Town Yacht Basin because there was no slip big enough to accommodate the boat inside. And he wasn't searching for anything but an expensive, first edition book. But love found both of them. The best thing is, Dirk and Oliver genuinely like each other, which makes doing things together super fun. Dirk has visited Oliver's sheep farm in England, and Oliver has done the San Francisco tourist thing with Dirk.

As we near the airport I can hardly sit still.

"Your face is flushed," Olivia says.

"So is yours," I tell her. We both look either feverish or like we're having a stroke.

The driver lets us out at the entrance to the airport and tells us where he'll be waiting. Olivia and I nervously stand on the pavement and inspect each other. To me, she looks perfect, and I tell her so. She shakes her head. "I can't wait to hear what Dirk says when he sees you. Don't be upset if he walks right past."

I'm too keyed up to let her remark annoy me. My heart is thudding in my chest as we watch the passengers come through Customs, and when I see him, my heart nearly stops beating. He looks wonderful—tall and tan and strong. I almost melt at the sight of his dark hair, sparkling blue eyes and fabulous smile. He spots Olivia, smiles and swings his eyes to me. The smile fades a bit, and he raises his brows questioningly.

Olivia was right. He doesn't recognize me. I race up to him waving my arms and yelling, "It's me."

He drops his carry on and wraps his arms around me. "I don't know what to say." He smiles. "Are you really my Julia?"

"Of course, I am." He smells so good. "I'm so happy to see you," I say into his chest.

"Me, too," he says into my hair. "I can't help staring at you. You look nice, but why are you dressed like this—sort of like the head mistress at a girl's school?"

"Really? I was going for another image."

"Whatever," he murmurs. "You can tell me all about it later. There will be plenty of time to talk."

I look over at Olivia, and she is similarly enveloped by Oliver. We laugh and chatter awkwardly as we walk through the airport and out to the car. Now that we're finally together, I can't seem to think of anything to say. I mean, so much has happened, but do I begin with "a man was stabbed to death at the house," or "someone has been trying to hurt me," or "the Kettani Ruby is missing, and for a while we worried Mal had something to do with it?" Instead I say, "Are you hungry? We can get something to eat at the hotel."

Dirk and Oliver have each reserved a suite at La Mamounia. Olivia and I are almost smug as we guide them through the almond milk and date check-in ritual. It seems to take forever until we're in our room, the cheerful employee has opened the drapes, explained how to use the house phone and served champagne.

When we're finally alone, Dirk holds me in a real hug and says, "So tell me everything. You have no idea how worried I've been about you. Let me see your head." He lifts the hair off my forehead and gently runs his finger over the healing wound. "That looks like it really hurt." He leads me to a purple velvet couch and says, "Let's sit down. Talk to me, Julia. What the heck is going on?"

I'm so glad to see him I'm almost crying, and I struggle to pull myself together. A tearstained face on a head mistress isn't a good look. "You have no idea how bizarre it's been," I begin. "I thought we came here to make key lime pies, but it's turned absolutely unreal."

"I want to hear everything, but first tell me something. Why does your hair feel like cement? I could scrape my knuckles knocking on it."

It will take me forever to explain. "Let's have lunch," I say, "and I can fill you in on all that's happened. "I'll wash this stuff out of my hair later, but right now I need it."

And at that moment, the phone in my pocket vibrates. Reluctantly, I answer and hear a breathless Mal say, "Thank heavens, I've caught you. M. Moreau is at the Mamounia right now. He's waiting to meet you in the Churchill bar."

"That's not very convenient, Mal. Dirk just got here, and we're about to go to lunch. Can't we meet later?" Dirk gives me a questioning look, and I give him a little smile.

"No, it has to be now. He said he has news about the Kettani Ruby. He actually said that. No more beating around the bush. Please, Julia. I'll never ask for another thing"

I glance at Dirk, who has wandered over to the balcony. "Listen, Mal, don't ask me to do this. Stall him or something. Let me repeat. Dirk just arrived."

"Julia, M. Moreau said he knows everything. This could be it. I'd go if I could, but you know I can't."

At the moment the last thing I care about is the Kettani Ruby, but Mal sounds frantic. I'm already regretting what I'm about to do.

Chapter 22

This should be the time Dirk and I are snuggled together catching up, but I'm so nervous about agreeing to meet M. Moreau, I can't sit still. I should be on my way to the bar, but I can't think of a way to tell Dirk I have to leave. For a while he pretends he doesn't notice but finally says, "Is everything okay? You seem kind of jumpy."

"I'm great. It's just that it's been hectic here and so much has happened, and I've missed you so much, and I'm so glad you're here."

Dirk smiles and points to my hands. I look down to see I've shredded a paper napkin into pieces, and the pieces are moist because my hands are sweating.

"I'm so sorry, Dirk." I toss the shreds into the wastebasket. "You must be exhausted after your trip. Why don't you take nap and we'll spend the afternoon chatting after you get some rest."

"You want me to sleep?" He grins. "Are you sleeping with me?"

"Ha ha. No, I have to run out for a minute, but I'll be right back."

"I thought we were having lunch."

"We will. As soon as I get back. I promise I won't be gone long."

Dirk is gazing out the window so it's hard to tell what he's thinking, but judging from the firm set of his jaw, I'm guessing he isn't pleased.

"I see. Hopefully you'll explain all this to me when you have time."

Oh my. This is starting so badly. "Dirk, I…"

"Go, Julia. I'm sure you have a very good reason. I'll find Olivia and Oliver and have lunch with them."

I grab my purse and jacket and head to the door. I can't look at Dirk, and I'm fighting hard to keep tears from flowing down my face.

The bar is dark and full of leather furniture. I can almost smell the lingering smoke from Winston Churchill's cigar. I find M. Moreau sitting at a table in a corner, and I plop down in a chair across from him.

"This has better be good. I'm missing an important appointment." I realize I don't sound like the snooty Stephanie Orca Wesley, but honestly, I don't care, and I don't have time for niceties.

"Ah, Madam Wesley, you seem somewhat stressed."

"Sorry about that. Let's get down to business. Tell me why you wanted to meet me."

"Would you care for a drink?"

"Thank you, I think not." I cross my arms across my chest and wait.

"Very well, madam. I have news about a certain ruby."

"What kind of news? Were you able to find what I'm looking for?"

He pushes aside his coffee cup and teepees his fingers. "Let us be plain. We are talking about the Kettani Ruby, are we not?"

"And if we are?"

"Are you aware it was stolen from the Kettani house?"

I don't answer because I don't know what to say. Better to keep quiet and look mysterious.

M. Moreau is beginning to squirm uncomfortably, so my silence is working.

"If I am incorrect, madam…"

"Go ahead."

"I should be able to have the ring in my possession very soon, but as I told you, it will be expensive. Extremely expensive."

"I assure you money doesn't matter."

"In that case, madam, would it be possible to have a small down payment? There are people I will have to pay."

This presents a dilemma because my bank balance is precariously low. The only jewelry I can afford is what I find in a souk. "I don't think that would be appropriate at this time. Perhaps if you could show me some proof of imminent possession, I'd be able to advance some money." I don't know how, but talk is cheap.

"It is in good hands." He bites his lower lip. "May I be indiscreet? I understand all is not well within the Kettani household. There are many rumors about the staff and family. Many very unsettling rumors. The ruby itself is probably cursed. Are you sure it is the one you want?"

"I'm sure. Curses don't bother me. I'd be interested to learn what rumors you've heard."

"Certainly, madam. I'll be happy to tell you—for a price. Surely we can come to some agreement."

This is an odious little man, and I have no intention of paying him, mostly because I don't have the money. "I'm not paying for gossip, M. Moreau. If you have verifiable information, please tell me." I change the subject. "Let me ask you something else. Did you bring the elephant pin?"

He looks disappointed. "I did, but why are you interested in such an insignificant piece? As I told you, the seller is requesting only $50,000." He reaches into a leather briefcase, pulls out a velvet pouch and dumps the pin on the table. "It is rather lovely, isn't it? This is genuine ivory, which no one is permitted to buy anymore."

The fake diamonds around the elephant's neck blink in the dark room. I pick it up and use the flashlight on my cell phone to examine the back. The M is clearly visible. This is Mal's pin. I put it back on the table and hope I look disgusted.

"M. Moreau, why are you trying to sell me a piece of costume jewelry? This isn't real ivory, and these are not diamonds."

He looks stunned. "Madam, I assure you this is a genuine piece. The seller assured me of that."

"Well, the seller is wrong. Did you look at it carefully?"

He finds his jeweler's loup in his briefcase, sticks it in his eye and examines the pin—for what seems like hours. He finally puts the pin down and folds his hands. "It seems, madam, I have made a significant mistake. You are indeed correct. This is not something I want in my inventory. I will discuss this with the seller."

He's about to toss it into his briefcase when I say, "I'd like to buy that trinket from you. It will amuse my cook."

"Very well, madam. Shall we say $500?"

"Let us say $30. I'm being generous, and I won't mention this to anyone, so your reputation will remain intact." I hope he agrees to this because I have exactly $33.27 in American dollars in my purse.

He hands me the pin and doesn't look happy. "I trust this matter will stay between us. As to the other, I need to know if we're in agreement. If I bring you proof I have the Kettani Ruby, you will purchase it?"

"Yes. Of course. But it must be soon. I won't be in Morocco much longer."

We both stand up, and he shakes my hand. "Au revoir, madam. I trust we will be seeing each other again very soon."

"I sincerely hope so, Monsieur Moreau. In fact, I'm counting on it. Bring me the Kettani Ruby, and you'll be a very wealthy man."

Lordy. I actually believe what I'm saying.

As soon as he's out of sight, I race back to our room. I burst through the door with a smile on my face, but the room is empty. No sign of Dirk, not even a note. I go onto the balcony and look down at the tables in the garden. Dirk, Olivia and Oliver are there, and they're talking and laughing. I wave at them, but they don't see me, and yelling at them doesn't seem appropriate. It seems Dirk doesn't miss me at all. Swell. I flop down on the bed and close my eyes. Maybe when I open them I'll have been teleported to a different dimension where there's no murder, intrigue or an angry lawyer from Sacramento.

It's dusk when I finally open my eyes and see I'm still in the room and Dirk is sitting at the desk working on his laptop. When he sees I'm awake, he comes over and sits on the edge of the bed.

"Are you feeling okay? You've been asleep for three hours." He smiles. "I'm the one who should have jet lag."

"I'm so sorry about everything. Can you forgive me?"

"Of course, I can. You're hard to stay mad at." He kicks off his shoes and stretches out next to me. "Now how about telling me what's been going on? Olivia tried, but what I could understand sounded terrible. Start at the beginning and don't leave anything out."

Dirk is an excellent, well known attorney in California, and he's used to listening to people. He's smiling when I begin to talk, but soon he's wearing his lawyer face, which means he's concerned. I tell him everything, and it sounds awful and improbable even to me. When I finish, he silently pulls me into a hug. I push away and look at him. "So what do you think?"

He pulls me back. "I think I'm glad I'm here. Until we leave, you aren't going anywhere without me."

I feel my body relax. Thank heavens. Now that I don't have to fight the bad guys by myself, I find I'm suddenly starving. We order *foie gras* with dates and almonds because Dirk wants to try it, then a lobster tagine with vegetables and a totally unnecessary but absolutely tantalizing rack of lamb. We sit on the balcony to eat until we are so full we can barely waddle. The night air is balmy and sweet, and in the distance the Koutoubia Mosque is a dark silhouette against the evening sky. When we hear the *muezzin* call the faithful to evening prayer, we go back into the room. "This is a beautiful place," Dirk says right before he closes the drapes.

Chapter 23

"I'm planning a little lunch by the pool with just a few people. We're so anxious to meet Lord Parker-Smythe and your friend."

I want to ask Vivian how she got my cell phone number and also remind her my friend's name is Dirk Harrison. "I don't think so, Vivian. We've made plans for today."

Olivia is shaking her head vigorously and mouthing, "Whatever it is, tell her no."

"Please reconsider your plans, Julia. I know Malika would be very pleased. The weather is so pleasant. We must take advantage of it."

I glance at Dirk, who's listening to my side of the conversation. I put my hand over the phone and ask, "Do you want to meet the inmates of the asylum?"

"I sure do. Can't wait."

"Well, I can," I assure him. "I'll go back there because you're here. Otherwise, never again. How about you, Olivia? Will you and Oliver go, too? Please? Actually you have to go. Oliver's the one she wants to see."

"I believe I'd enjoy meeting this person," Oliver says. "I've heard so much about her." His tongue in cheek remark makes us all smile. I'm afraid Olivia and I haven't given her glowing reviews.

"Okay, Vivian," I say into the phone. "We'll come, but we can't stay long."

"Excellent. Will you also extend the invitation to His Lordship?"

"If you mean Oliver Parker-Smythe, I'll try to convey the message."

"Thank you, Julia. Shall we say 12:30?"

I agree and end the call. "Well, that ruins a perfectly nice morning."

The four of us are sitting on our balcony enjoying coffee, pastries and fruit. Oliver offers a slice of mango to Olivia. "This should be interesting. I can't wait to meet all the characters in this mystery."

I laugh. "See if you can still say that in a few hours. I sure don't want to go back to that house. I've had enough mystery and intrigue."

"I'm very curious about the missing ruby ring," Dirk says. "I'd be willing to bet it's still around here somewhere. A piece like that would be extremely difficult to sell or fence."

This makes me remember what Aziz said about the man in the house outside of Marrakech. Mal was so eager to visit him. I wonder if she went by herself.

"I'm sorry," Mal whispers to me as we enter the house. "Vivian absolutely insisted. I tried to tell her you and Olivia had other plans."

"It's okay. Don't worry about it." I point to her shoulder and smile. "I love your pin." She's wearing the elephant pin I returned to her. “Has anyone mentioned it?”

“No, but I could see Vivian looking at it. She seems to be in a bit of a flap today.”

The lady of the house has gone all out to impress His Lordship. Colorful umbrellas protect the white tables from the blazing sun. Hundreds of fragrant pink rose petals float in the pool. I wonder how many rosebushes were denuded to create this extravaganza. Young women carry a steady stream of platters and dishes to a buffet table. The folks from our Sahara adventure are here, as well as Corey Fieldstone and his wife, Belle. Vivian flutters among us trying to be the perfect hostess. Dirk and Oliver are having an animated conversation with the Bouchers, and to my utter astonishment, it is all in French. When Dirk sees me staring at him, he says in my ear, “My grandmother was from Lyon. I learned French as a kid.”

Honestly, does everyone in the world know how to speak this language? I can see Corey hovering behind us, dying for a chance to talk to Oliver. I’m kind of interested to see that myself. We have warned Oliver, and it will be like watching a cat toy with a mouse.

When Corey finally sees an opening, he pounces. “It’s such a pleasure to meet you, Your Lordship. Such an honor. I’ve read so many articles about your philanthropy and your successful sheep farm. I’d certainly love to see it.”

“I’m afraid we’re not open to the public,” Oliver politely tells him.

I’m smiling to myself because I know Corey doesn’t like being referred to as “the public.” He wants to be an invited guest.

I’m wondering when we’re going to eat when I feel a tap on my shoulder. Vivian attempts a smile. “Would you have a minute to chat with me? I’m sorry if I’ve seemed…ah…somewhat brisk in the past. I’ve been terribly worried about things.”

As we talk, we walk down the length of the pool to a small bench. She sits and pats the space next to her. I shake my head. I'll stand to hear what she has to say. When I decline to sit, she gets up and we resume walking.

"I'm sure Malika told you the Kettani Ruby is missing. We've all been terribly upset about this as you can assuredly understand." She hesitates. "I don't know if you're aware of this, but she fancied herself a good friend of Fatima, Kadem's first wife."

I stop walking. "Are you saying she wasn't?"

"My dear, I'm simply saying my step-daughter has a vivid imagination. She certainly knew Fatima, but were they close? I think that would be terribly improbable. Fatima was a lovely, gracious woman. She would have been kind to Nabil's wife, but I cannot picture them as confidantes. I don't know what Malika has been saying, but I know she's been searching high and low for the ring. She seems obsessed with finding it, which I find somewhat puzzling. After all, she isn't a Kettani by birth and has no claim to the ring. It belongs to Kadem. As I mentioned before, Malika needs funds. Perhaps that's the reason she's searching so diligently." She pauses. "I'm wondering if you've been helping her." She puts a warm hand on my arm. "Please don't misunderstand me. I think it's wonderful Malika has a good friend. She needs a strong, sensible person like you to keep her from spiraling out of control."

Whoa! Spiraling out of control? I've never seen any sign of out of control spiraling.

"Anyway," she continues, "Have you girls been able to find anything?" She gives me a fake smile. "I hope you would confide in me. Together we can protect Malika if need be."

This is interesting. Vivian is asking what I know, and I'm not going to tell her. "I'm sure I don't know what you mean. Olivia and I were guests in your home. We certainly wouldn't abuse your hospitality by snooping. I can tell you, though, if I did find anything, I would take the information straight to Kadem."

"There would be no need to bother him with this. He's a busy man. If you do have any information, I'd be grateful if you'd share it with me." Her voice is no longer dripping with honey.

"One more thing, Vivian. You implied Malika might need protection. Why?"

"It's obvious, isn't it, my dear. Whoever took the ring might be dangerous. But as I said, your friend sometimes lives in a fantasy land. She is not enjoying life here in our beautiful country, so who knows what she conjures up in her unhappy mind, and who knows what she says. We can control her imagined close relationship with Fatima, but what if she begins to talk about hunting for the ring. Maybe she says she even has leads. People might hurt her."

"That's a frightening thought, Vivian, and I think you've greatly misjudged Malika."

She gives me a pitying look. "You Americans are so naïve. All I can say, Julia, is I hope your friend watches her back. And I hope you do, too."

When we finally sit down to lunch, I glance at my phone. We've already been here one hour and seventeen minutes. My conversation with Vivian has made me lose my appetite and now all I want to do is eat fast and get out. The food, however, might be a reason to linger. It is fantastic—a bit heavy for lunch, perhaps—but absolutely delicious. There's a quiche-like concoction of eggs, vegetables and spices, a platter of hot, perfectly seasoned meat, fresh dates and mangos, a wonderful array of breads and pastries, mint tea and coffee. I know Suad has prepared this, and I intend to go to the kitchen and tell her how much we loved it.

I look around the table, listening to the conversation. Corey has given up trying to impress Oliver and has turned his attention to Dirk.

"I considered becoming a lawyer," I hear him say, "but I decided law school wasn't for me. Too structured. I prefer the freedom to be flexible. Move with the wind. Explore life's adventures. I pity you lawyers, always stuck in offices."

Corey should stop talking. Lawyers certainly aren't stuck in offices, but Dirk is too nice to contradict him. "I'm glad you're happy with your life," he says.

I feel a bit sorry for Corey. He's trying so hard. I wonder about Belle, his wife. She hasn't said much and seems to be concentrating on a warm piece of bread.

Oliver, who's sitting next to me, leans over and speaks softly. "I'm confused about Vivian. I know her village in the Cotswold well. I have a little thatched roof house not far from where she said she lived. There's an absolutely marvelous restaurant in the village, and everyone in the area knows about it. I asked Vivian if she enjoyed the food there, and she looked at me blankly for a second, then laughed and said 'Of course. I always enjoy their beef Wellington.'"

I put a hunk of lovely bread on my plate. "So what's wrong with that?"

"The restaurant is called Le Petit Lapin. They only serve rabbit. It's their specialty. Everyone knows that. They definitely do not serve beef Wellington."

"Maybe she confused this place with another one."

"Not possible. There's no other restaurant."

I stop eating and turn to Oliver. "Are you saying you think she didn't really live in the Cotswold? Why would she lie about that?"

"I have no idea, Julia. I don't know the lady. But there's something not quite right about her. She told me she was heavily involved with a charity I know well. When I mentioned the chairperson, she acted like she'd never heard of her. Yet she tried to get me to invest in a cause dear to her. I told her no because I've never heard of it. She wanted a substantial amount."

"What!" I know my voice is too loud because several people stop eating and turn around. "This is too much. She can't solicit money from my friends."

"Who can't solicit money?" Olivia comes over and stands behind us. "What were you yelling about, Julia?"

"You won't believe what Oliver just told me, but that can wait. Are you finished eating? I want to show Dirk the garden."

The four of us walk around the pool and down the path. Olivia and I point out where the knife was found, and we show them the fountain and the area with the broken branches. The piece of fabric we saw in the fountain is gone. As we round a corner near the rosebushes, we almost collide with Corey Fieldstone, who's sticking his cell phone in his pocket. And he looks embarrassed.

"I decided I needed a little exercise after that lunch. I didn't know you folks were out here."

"And we didn't know you were here," I say.

I expect him to fall into step with us, so he can schmooze some more with Dirk and Oliver, but instead he makes his excuses and scurries away.

I shake my head. "That was odd."

Olivia agrees. "He must have been talking on his phone and having a conversation he didn't want anyone to hear."

Dirk puts his arm around my waist. "We'll never know. Come on. Introduce me to the lady who cooked the wonderful meal."

Suad is busy at the sink, but her face lights up when she sees us, and her smile is even broader when she realizes Dirk can speak French. I listen while the two talk and once again vow to learn this language. It's going to be number one on my 'To Do list.' When they finally stop chatting, Dirk grins at me and says, "This is a lovely lady, and she sure likes you."

"Can you please tell her I like her, too. And tell her how sensational the food was."

Once again I wait and am puzzled when Dirk's face creases in a frown. "I don't know what this is all about, but she said she heard Jamal will be at his house tonight." He pauses. "She also says she heard he has the Kettani Ruby. And she thinks she's also in danger. Someone searched her room, and a man threatened to cut her if she told anyone her suspicions."

This is horrible. How on earth has this situation spiraled so out of control? While Dirk is talking, Suad is tugging urgently at my arm, trying to tell me something. "She wants you to go there and talk to Jamal." The anguished look on Suad's face tears at my soul. She is genuinely terrified. "I don't like this, Julia. This isn't something we should be involved in, and there's no way on earth I'd let you go meet this Jamal by yourself. You're not thinking of doing that, are you?"

It certainly doesn't sound appealing, but it would be great if I could find the ring and end this drama. I mean, what could happen to me? I'm an American.

"I can hear you thinking," Dirk says. "You might as well say it out loud, and I don't think American citizenship will save you."

"Maybe we could just have a little look. I'm sure we wouldn't be in any danger. After all, we're tourists in this country."

"Your logic makes my brain hurt. I think we should leave this alone. I know you're very fond of Suad, but this isn't our business."

"I'd sort of like to do this, Dirk. We go home in a few days, so

I'm sure we'll be okay. Just a quick chat with this man."

"Again, your reasoning is astounding. What does going home have to do with anything? If you insist on doing this, I'm going with you."

"Not necessary," I say primly. He's beginning to make me mad.

"Really? What if he only speaks French. But I'm sure you can handle that."

He has me there. "Okay. A quick, perfectly harmless visit and we'll be back on the balcony of our room in no time. You'll see. It will be fine."

He scowls. "Stop saying that. Do you know how to find this place?"

"Oh yes! It's a little village on the left side of the main road out of Marrakech. There are lots of goats, and his house only has one window."

He actually rolls his eyes and turns to Suad, who is able to give him accurate directions—and the keys to her car.

Chapter 24

Things are a bit frosty between Dirk and me. He thinks I'm crazy, and I honestly can't blame him, but he hasn't been hit on the head and assaulted in a souk. I want to find the person responsible for my headaches. And I'm not trying to be a flake. I'm well aware my directions to this village were—let's say creative—but I was working with what I'd been given. I guess you have to have been here for all the trouble to understand why I want to talk to this guy. Finding an end to all this would be terrific.

It's a pleasant drive as long as we're in Marrakech, but once we leave the city, the road is plunged into darkness. Dirk doesn't say much as he concentrates on Suad's directions, and I'm wishing Olivia and Oliver were with us. There's safety in numbers plus Oliver is a big strong intimidating guy. But they're meeting an old friend of Oliver's at a restaurant this evening.

"Do you know where you're going?" I ask timidly. Dirk and I aren't chatting much. We speak if spoken to, but that's about it.

"I have my fingers crossed. I tried to find this place on my phone app, but no luck."

"Thank you for doing this. I know you don't want to, but it's important to me."

He reaches across the seat and takes my hand. "I hope you know I always have your back. I'm just worried you're going to get hurt."

I feel tears spring to my eyes. He is such a good guy. "We'll laugh about this when we're back home." He doesn't answer.

We drive in silence until Dirk points out the window and says, "I think that's it. It has to be. There's nothing else around here."

I see the silhouettes of low adobe structures. There are no lights so it's impossible to tell if there are any goats. Dirk pulls off the road onto the dirt and kills the engine.

"I think the house we're looking for is the one over there on the left."

I'm suddenly very uneasy. "What should we do? It's terribly dark." I'm trying to ignore a persistent feeling in my gut telling me this is a stupid idea, and we need to go back to the hotel and eat something decadent. Another thought occurs to me. "What if he has a gun? Do you have one with you?"

In the dark I can feel him staring at me. "You're kidding, right" Where on earth would I get a gun?"

I sink down in the seat. "Maybe we should just get out of here."

"Nope. We're here so we're going to find this guy, hear what he knows and hope this ends the drama once and for all."

"I can't do it. I'm scared."

"I'd like to tell you there's nothing to be afraid of, but that wouldn't be accurate. I have no idea what we're walking into."

This does nothing to reassure me. In fact, I feel worse. We sit without talking until Dirk says, "Come on, Julia. Pull up your socks and let's go. I see a flicker of light, which must be coming from an oil lamp. These people don't have electricity."

I climb out of the car and try to pull myself together. "At least we know they're not sitting around watching TV." I'm trying to make a joke, but my mouth is dry, and I can feel my heart beating fast. "Maybe we should get back in the car."

"Nope. Let's do this. We'll find Jamal, and then hopefully we'll finally have some time to ourselves."

"Once again I'm sorry," I tell him. "Olivia and I came to Marrakech to make key lime pies. I never in a million years imagined we'd get involved in all this."

He squeezes my hand. "I know you didn't intend for this to happen, but it really doesn't surprise me. In Iceland someone tried to kill you by pushing you off a building, and on the Alaska cruise the bad guy locked you in a refrigerated box in the ship's morgue. And remember the demented man who kidnapped you on Hilton Head Island? I love you dearly, but you attract trouble. At least now you're with me, and I promise you I'm not going to let anyone try to kill you."

I sure hope that's true. I turn around and follow Dirk to the house.

"What do we do now? Do we knock?" I plaster myself against Dirk's solid frame. It's scary dark out here, and there are noises I don't recognize.

"What are you going to say?" he asks. "You probably shouldn't start with demanding the Kettani Ruby."

My body is shaking like a palm tree in a hurricane. "I definitely think this is a bad idea. Let's get back in the car."

"Too late for that now. We came here to find Jamal, and that's what we're going to do."

While we're discussing how dumb this whole thing might be, the door opens, and a man comes out. He's wearing the traditional long white tunic and sandals on his feet. Behind him in the dim light I see a woman dressed all in black sitting on the floor. A little girl runs toward us, and when she sees we're not Moroccan runs back to the woman. Thank heavens, Dirk is here because I seem to be incapable of speech. I tried, but the words came out as an unintelligible squeak.

Dirk is talking, and I don't know exactly what he's saying, but I recognize the word 'Jamal.' There's more conversation, which may not be going well because the man moves threateningly close to Dirk. Dirk, who's not a timid or small man, stands his ground. There are angry words exchanged until Dirk finally turns to me and says, "This is Jamal and he's also a punk. I told him we wanted to talk about the Kettani Ruby and he went off like a rocket. I don't think we're going to learn anything from him."

While Dirk is speaking, I have my eyes on the man, so I'm the first one to see the glint of a knife in his hand. I yell, "Look out, Dirk. He has a knife," and the events that followed happened so fast, it's hard to remember everything. Jamal puts his hand on Dirk's chest in an attempt to push him back. Dirk grabs Jamal's wrist and says in English, "Back off, man. We only came to talk."

This idea doesn't seem to appeal to Jamal. He lunges at Dirk, Dirk neatly sidesteps, and I'm frankly terrified. Jamal stumbles onto the dirt, turns around and attempts to throw Dirk to the ground. In the darkness, I see the flash of the knife as Jamal raises it above his head. Without thinking, I aim a kick at Jamal's arm, which must have landed successfully because I hear a yelp and the clink of metal against a rock. Then I jump on Jamal's back and try to haul him off my guy. He shakes me off as if I'm a troublesome fly, and I land on my butt in the dirt.

"I've got this, Julia," I hear Dirk say. "Stay out of the way."

When I scramble to my feet, I see Dirk has tied Jamal's hands behind his back with zip ties and has forced him to a sitting position. "Now let's find out what he knows."

"I'm not talking to you," Jamal snarls.

Startled, we look at our captive. "You speak English?"

"So what."

"So it makes it easier," Dirk says. "My friend here will be able to understand you."

"What's that to me?"

Dirk sighs. "Look, pal. All we want to do is talk. We don't care what you've done or what you're up to now. We just have a few questions and would like some answers. Or if you prefer, I can use my cell phone right now to call the police. I'll say I'm an American tourist and you've assaulted the lady and me. How do you think that will work out for you? Or we can have a friendly chat, you can go back to your family, and we'll be on our way. Which is it?"

It doesn't take Jamal long to answer. "What do you want to know?"

"Excellent. First of all, your English is very good. How long were you in the States? And where?"

"Ten months in New York and Pennsylvania."

"What were you doing there?"

"Visiting my sick aunt," he growls. "None of your business."

"What's your relation to the Kettani family?"

"Who?"

I can tell Dirk is getting annoyed. I'm also getting a glimpse of his lawyer skills. I'd hate to have him peppering me with questions, but I have one of my own.

"Where did you get the zip ties, Dirk? I mean, most people don't have them in their pocket."

"Julia, can you please focus. I'll explain about the zip ties later." To Jamal he says, "Are you saying you don't have any connection to the Kettani family? Think carefully."

Silence.

"Let's try this. What do you know about the Kettani ruby ring?" When Jamal still doesn't answer, Dirk pulls out his phone. "Okay, have it your way. I can see this isn't going to work."

"Someone took the ring from the Kettani house, and no one knows where it is."

"Good choice. Keep talking. Who could have taken the ring? Someone on the staff?"

"We would know if someone from the staff took it. It's said the safe holding the ring was impossible to break open. But someone was able. I don't know who, and now it's disappeared."

"This is interesting," Dirk says, "because the rumor is you have it."

"If I had it, I wouldn't be sitting here." Jamal's voice is flat and ugly.

"Who are you working for, Jamal? I assume you're not in this by yourself."

Silence, and I can tell Dirk is just about finished being nice. "Look Jamal. I'm not playing games anymore, and I promise you I'll have no problem calling the police. So once again I'm asking you, who are you working for?"

"I'm working for a jeweler."

His voice is almost a whisper, but I hear him and yell, "Ah ha! Is it M. Moreau?"

Even in the dark,, I can tell Jamal is startled. "How do you know about him?"

"Never mind how she knows," Dirk says. "Can we assume you've promised the ring to him once you have it in your possession? He'll pay you a substantial amount and then…"

"You're so smart, you figure it out," Jamal snarls.

"…M. Moreau will sell it to someone."

I tap Dirk on the shoulder. "Ask him if he killed Abdul."

"No!" The words burst out of Jamal's mouth. "And I swear I

don't know who did. No one knows."

"Back to M. Moreau," Dirk says. "How did you know he was trying to buy the ring?"

"Everyone knows that. The word is out, and we are all looking for it. It would be impossible for one of us to sell it because it is so well known, but a jeweler can do many things. He can take it apart and sell the ruby and diamonds separately. He has offered a large reward to the person who brings it to him."

"But Monsieur Kettani is offering a reward, too," I interject. "Why not just give it to him?"

"Bah!" Jamal spits on the ground to emphasize his disgust. "The reward he is offering is insignificant. And we don't trust that family." He points at me. "We thought you had knowledge of the ring because of your close ties to Mme. Kettani. Then we thought Aziz had it because he is also close to the family. We had to keep an eye on him."

An idea occurs to me. "So no one was following Mme. Kettani? The man was actually following Aziz?"

"Yes, but it turns out he doesn't have it either or knows where it is."

"Who is this "we" you keep mentioning?" Dirk asks.

"There are many of us—people who work for the Kettanis and others. We all know the ring is here somewhere. We just have to find it."

"You speak as if you're from this village, Jamal, but we know you're not." I see Dirk rub his shoulder and wonder if he got hurt in the scuffle. "Why are you here?"

"That's a foolish question," Jamal answers. "I'm here to find the ring and become rich."

Dirk pulls Jamal to his feet. Before he cuts off the zip ties, he says, "One last question. Who's supposed to have the ruby now? There must be a rumor."

"It is said Youssef has it, but I don't recommend asking him. He's mean, and rumor has it he has killed a man."

"You mean he killed Abdul?" I ask.

"No." In the darkness I can feel him looking at me. "You foreigners have no idea. We don't kill our own."

"And where would we find this Youssef?"

"In the Jemaa el Fna. In the meat stall. He sells sheep heads and parts, but he won't talk to you because he doesn't like Americans."

Swell. It just keeps getting better and better.

Chapter 25

It is evening, and the Jemaa el Fna is alive with activity. Light from the overhead lanterns dance across the square, giving the scene a magical glow. The open markets of the day have been replaced with food stalls everywhere, and the tantalizing smoke from grills smells wonderful. The snake charmers are there, as are the story tellers. Fortune tellers are doing a brisk business, and people are dancing to the live music.

Oliver and Dirk are amazed. "I've never seen anything like this," Oliver says. "The whole place is quite intoxicating."

Dirk agrees. "I can't wait to explore more."

I sigh. Really? This is the last place I wanted to visit. Up until now the day has been perfect. The four of us sat by the pool, ate great food, and for the first time in days, totally relaxed. We didn't mention Abdul, the Kettani Ruby or murder even once but being here in the square brings it all back.

"Let's find this person and get out of here," I say. "One quick stroll around the place and we're done. Agreed?"

Dirk puts his arm around my waist and grins. "Are we in a

hurry? This is fascinating. I'd like to see more."

"We should look for Youssef's stall," I insist. "It can't be that hard to find someone selling sheep's heads."

It turns out I'm wrong. Judging by the number of heads prominently displayed in the stalls, it's obvious that Youssef doesn't have a monopoly on this product, and the sight of all those bodiless heads is making me queasy.

Dirk points to one of the stalls. "We're never going to find him wandering around. I think we should sit down and order something. Then we can ask if Youssef is there."

Oliver nods. "I'd actually like to try it. If prepared correctly it can be quite tasty."

Is he kidding? I don't want to, but I allow myself to be propelled to a long table accommodating many diners. I squeeze into a seat next to a man either enjoying his meal or experiencing gastric distress because he keeps rubbing his belly. I'm having gastric distress when I see the cook pull a huge head out of a boiling pot of liquid, whack it with a meat cleaver and put bits of meat and whatever on our plates. It looks gruesome, and I swear I see a tooth. Even Oliver, who up until now has been rubbing his hands in anticipation, has turned an alarming shade of pale.

I push my plate away. "Sorry, folks. I just can't do this. I realize different cultures, different foods, but this is disgusting."

"I'm with her," Olivia says. "Can't we just ask for Youssef?"

We both look pointedly at Oliver, who is pushing the sheep's head's bits and pieces around with a piece of bread. "Okay, you win. I'm not all that hungry. Otherwise, I'd be devouring this."

Thank heavens. We stand up and send Oliver to ask the cook for information about Youssef. He comes back shaking his head. "He doesn't know a Youssef and seemed annoyed we didn't enjoy our food. We should move on."

We venture into another stall that sells not only sheep's heads but other food as well. We sit down and order *harira*, a wonderful soup made of tomatoes, chick peas, lentils, lamb and spices.

"This is more like it," I say. "Much more civilized."

I keep my eyes on my soup and try to ignore the man next to me eating a sheep's head. When I finish my food and the contents of my stomach are still where they belong, I conclude I'm becoming a bit used to local customs.

This time, Dirk pays the bill and asks about Youssef. "The man said, 'down there' and pointed to an area at the end of the square," he tells us.

"That's hopeful," I say. "At least we know he's here somewhere."

"Youssef is a common name," Dirk tells me. "There could be many men named Youssef here."

We try more stalls without success, then deviate from our mission because Oliver is fascinated by a snake charmer. For a few dirham, the snake charmer allows us to photograph him holding the snake's head close to his mouth. The snake is flicking its tongue and does not look pleased.

"These men believe they have divine protection," Dirk whispers to me. "Maybe they do since they don't get bitten—very often."

I hope that's true because the snake is making a valiant effort to score a chunk of the man's nose.

"Again, different cultures, different customs. We don't have this in Wake Forest." I back up against Dirk because the grinning snake charmer is walking toward me holding the reptile out in front. And Oliver is grinning, too.

"He's going to put the snake around your neck, Julia, and we'll take a picture. This will make a great souvenir."

"I think not," I say, putting my hand out. "No way, no how." But no one is listening. The snake charmer, who's a foot shorter than I am, missing several teeth and smiling broadly, hangs the wretched reptile around my neck and snuggles next to me for the photo. The snake is surprisingly heavy, and I must have divine protection, too, because it doesn't try to bite me. But enough is enough. I wriggle out from the snake and say, "We need to carry on with our mission—that is, to find Youssef."

The snake charmer puts his reptile pal into a basket and accepts more money. We're stunned when he says, in perfect English, "You are looking for a Youssef?"

"We are, indeed," Dirk confirms. "The man we are looking for sells sheep's heads."

"Then you want to go past the next three stands, take a right at the sausage stall, and continue until you almost reach the end of the food area. You'll find him on the right. He's a big man who sweats a lot and has gray hair. I'd advise being careful. He's not a friendly man."

We have no opportunity to ask this amazing man where he learned English because our jaws are hanging open and by the time we close them, the articulate snake charmer has melted into the crowd. We follow his directions and actually find the stall. The man is there, he's sweaty and has scraggly gray hair that shoots out in all directions. He's also wearing an apron smeared with blood and is wielding what could pass for a samurai sword to crack open the sheep's heads.

"So, what are we going to do?" I ask. "He looks busy. Maybe we shouldn't bother him."

Oliver shakes his head. "We've come this far. It would be ridiculous to turn away now."

I disagree. "This man can't possibly have the ring. If he did, he surely wouldn't be working here."

As I try to convince the others to leave, Dirk goes into the stall and sits down at a table. He speaks to the cleaver-wielding man, smiles and motions for us to join him, which I try to ignore, but Olivia and Oliver take a seat at the table, so I have no choice.

"This will be much easier," he says. "Our new friend speaks passable English."

Dirk orders tea and French fries, which are actually quite good, and we watch for a chance to talk to the man, but he's busy with customers. We eat slowly and linger over our tea until he begins to glare at us.

"We should leave," I tell the others. "Our Youssef doesn't look happy."

"No, he doesn't," Dirk says. "We've probably stayed here too long. I'd still like to have a word with him, though."

Dirk is much braver than I am. We all stand up, and Olivia and I head for open spaces, but Oliver and Dirk approach Youssef. I see Dirk say something and Youssef, thankfully, puts down his knife, but out of the corner of my eye I see something else. I see a man standing at the edge of the stall, and I'm shocked to realize I know this person. It is Monsieur Moreau.

I grab Olivia's arm and point. "Do you see what I see?"

"I do. What do you suppose he's doing here?"

"I'd be willing to bet it has something to do with the Kettani ruby. He's obviously waiting to talk to Youssef." I trot toward the man, pulling Olivia with me.

"Yoo hoo! Monsieur Moreau! A word?"

Startled, he turns around to see who's yelling. Apparently, two women running through the square is alarming because he backs into the stall, which makes talking to him much easier.

"I'm sorry, madam. Do I know you?"

I'm not all glammed up like I was for our first meeting, but I stick out my hand and say, "Stephanie Orca Wesley here."

He stares at me in disbelief. "Really?"

"Really. Surely I don't look that different."

By now Dirk, Oliver and Youssef have heard the commotion and joined us. I quickly make the introductions, and it's obvious Youssef and the jeweler know each other. And M. Moreau is still staring.

"You're Madam Wesley? The lady with the diamond?"

"Yes, I left my diamond ring in my other purse." I glance at Dirk, who's trying very hard not to laugh.

Dirk steps forward and says, "We're interested in buying the Kettani ruby ring, and we understand one of you has it. Is that an accurate statement?"

M. Moreau and Youssef exchange looks and some kind of secret signal because M. Moreau nods. "We have it, and it will be available for purchase tomorrow morning."

I inhale sharply and my knees almost buckle. We're going to recover the fabled Kettani ring. Halleluiah!

"Excellent. What is your price, and where can we examine it?"

"We will have the ring here tomorrow morning at 10:00 and you may examine it in our presence. We will meet in the leather stall, which is run by Youssef's younger brother. We will be able to talk privately there. The price is17,000,000 US dollars." He states the price matter-of-factly as if we were negotiating for a pound of butter. "With all apologies for my rudeness, gentlemen, I don't know you. I've only had dealings with Madam Wesley. Therefore, she's the only one I will deal with. I hope you understand."

"I would advise you to allow me to attend with her," Dirk says. "I'm her husband, and I have the money."

Oh my. For the second time in a few minutes I suck in air and almost collapse.

I'm so excited I can hardly sit still. The four of us are on our balcony at the Mamounia discussing the day, and my heart is still beating wildly. I know Dirk said he was my husband only to convince M. Moreau to let him come with me to buy the ring, but I'm astounded at how happy the thought makes me. And since dinner at the Square was less than satisfying, we've ordered room service and are eating a delicious chicken and vegetable dish.

Olivia pushes her plate away. "I can't believe I'm saying this, but I think I miss Little Bites. You make good food, Julia. My stomach is beginning to rebel against all this rich fare. I think I could go a month without eating."

"I think I agree with you. My stomach actually hurts, but I've tried to ignore it. When we get home we'll have to do a cleanse. Nothing but veggies and broth." I turn to Dirk and say, "Are we actually going to buy this ring? I mean, how can we do that?"

"I'm assuming we wouldn't be expected to produce that kind of money on the spot," Oliver says. "We'd sign an agreement to purchase and then funds would be wired. But we don't have to worry about that. Don't forget the Kettani Ruby has been stolen. These folks are thieves. We're simply going to return it to its rightful owner."

"That's the way it would be done if this were a legal transaction," Dirk interrupts. "But it isn't. These people will want cash and no record of bank transfers."

"They'll expect us to show up with a suitcase full of money?" I ask. "That sounds impossible."

Dirk laughs. "As I said, don't worry about it. We're not going to buy it. We're going to take it from them."

It's now 10:37 at night, and Dirk, Olivia, Oliver and I are sitting in Mal's cozy office. "This is the only place we can talk with a degree of privacy. I can't wait to hear what you have to tell me," she says.

We tell her everything, and when Dirk says he's going to pretend to be my husband, I see Mal's eyebrows lift ever so slightly. I try to keep the expression on my face neutral.

"We need to know everything you can tell us about the ring; the carat weight of the ruby, the setting, the clarity and carat weight of the diamonds surrounding it. Also any identifying marks," Oliver says. "And pictures. Pictures would be helpful."

Mal disappears for a few minutes, and when she returns, she's holding the green folder we saw in her hiding hole in the former master bedroom.

"That goon Brandon is patrolling the halls. He actually had the nerve to ask me where I was going. Anyway, here's all the information I have about the ring. You're welcome to take it with you. There's a small identification mark that Fatima told me about. The Kettanis were big on marking their valuable jewelry so there could be no question about authenticity. On the inside of the platinum setting there is a very tiny F etched in the metal. You have to know it's there to see it, and it certainly wouldn't be noticed by a casual observer."

I take the folder and give Mal a hug. "This is exciting. I really hope this time tomorrow we're celebrating the return of the famous Kettani Ruby."

"So this is the plan," Dirk says. "As soon as we have the ring in our possession and Oliver verifies it's the real deal, I'm going to take it and tell them we've called the police. There's only one problem. To do this, I probably need a gun. I certainly won't shoot anyone, but they don't know that." He looks at Mal. "Would you happen to have one we can borrow?"

Mal opens a drawer and pulls out a lethal looking revolver. "Will this do? I'm sure we have more in the house if you'd rather have something else." The gun is small and fits in the palm of Dirk's hand. "Don't let its size fool you," Mal warns. "It's small, but it will still kill somebody."

Dirk grins. "This will do nicely. I'm not going to shoot

anybody, so we don't need bullets."

"Well, you probably shouldn't be waving it around," Mal advices. "I'm pretty sure it's loaded."

Chapter 26

It's still early in the morning, but the souk is already bustling with activity. Merchants are opening their stalls, and shoppers are buying fresh fruit and vegetables. When we made our plan we hadn't figured on a crowd, so this is going to make our getaway with the ring more perilous.

Before we reach the leather stall, Dirk pulls me aside. "Oliver and I have been talking, and we think it would be better if you carry the gun—just until you can give it back to me. These guys might pat us down looking for weapons. After all, they're criminals so they're not going to take chances. But they won't touch a woman. Oliver's going to examine the ring, and while he's doing that, you can slip the gun to me. Just stand close and when I give you the signal, put it in my pocket."

Is he nuts? I don't want to have anything to do with that gun. I shake my head. "This doesn't sound like a good plan. Think of something else."

"Listen, Julia. We don't have time to discuss this. They won't bother you because they think you're the wealthy Madam Wesley married to the fabulously wealthy Monsieur Wesley. They think I have all the money, and they won't jeopardize their chances of getting it by attempting to search you. You'll be perfectly safe."

Someone probably said, "This ship is new. We'll be perfectly safe," as passengers boarded the Titanic, but Dirk is right. We don't have time to argue. He reaches into his pocket, palms the revolver and slips it to me. The metal is cold in my hand, and I want to drop it on the ground but instead stick it in the pocket of my jacket. It feels heavy and noticeable, and I cover it with my shoulder bag.

We reach the leather stall and take a collective deep breath as we enter. A thick cloud of nasty cigarette smoke hangs over two men sitting at a table. They're drinking tea and talking. They glance briefly at us and go back to their cigarettes and beverages. A young boy is sitting on the ground fashioning a sandal out of pieces of leather. There's no sign of Youssef or M. Moreau.

This seemed like a good idea last night when, fueled by alcohol, we made our plan, but now in the cold light of morning —not so much. We're four Americans surrounded by many people in the souks who may not react kindly to Dirk snatching the ring from one of their own. Even if he does manage to run out of the stall, how far is he going to get before someone tackles him? In my mind I can already hear voices yelling, "Stop that man! in French, Arabic, English and whatever else works. I'm convincing myself we've made a mistake.

"Maybe we should rethink this," I say. "I don't see Youssef or M. Moreau. They must be having second thoughts, too."

But as I speak, the two men appear from the rear of the stall and nod to the men at the table, who get up and leave. Now that we're alone, they look at us expectantly.

"Show time," Dirk says softly. "Let's do this."

M. Moreau steps forward and puts out his hand to stop us.

"We said we would deal with you and your wife. These other two were not invited. Why are they here?"

Dirk puts his arm around Oliver's shoulder. "This man is my financial advisor. I don't make any major purchases without his input. You can trust him to be discreet. And surely you recognize Salma, my wife's assistant."

M. Moreau sighs and looks at Youssef, who also sighs. "I don't understand you people. You look quite different today." He straightens his back. "Nevertheless, this was not in our agreement. I hope you understand, but we must now search your bodies for weapons."

"Completely understandable," Dirk says casually.

My hands are so sweaty I surreptitiously try to wipe them off on my pants. I look at Olivia, who seems to be equally sweaty. It's almost impossible to appear unconcerned and pretend to admire a row of brown sandals on a shelf when I know my fingers can curl around the trigger of a loaded gun. Youssef pats down Dirk and Oliver and finding nothing, tells them to have a seat. I'm so aware of the revolver in my pocket, it feels like it's burning my skin.

"May we proceed?" Dirk asks. "Our time is limited as we're leaving Morocco soon."

"You have the money?"

"Obviously not on our persons, M. Moreau. We're not amateurs. Show us the ring and we'll produce the funds."

Youssef disappears into the back and returns carrying—almost reverently—a black velvet pouch. He pushes the full ashtrays aside and puts the pouch on the table. I can't help but notice how dirty his fingernails are. We all suck in our breath as M. Moreau opens the pouch and pulls out something carefully wrapped in cotton. It takes an agonizingly long time for him to peel off the cotton and deposit the object on top of the velvet pouch. We all lean forward for a first glimpse of the famous ring. And there it is. We are finally looking at the fabulous Kettani Ruby.

And it looks magnificent. The red ruby gleams in the center with flashing diamonds surrounding it. For a few minutes, no one says a word. M. Moreau is the first to speak. "I assume this is satisfactory and concludes our part of the transaction. May we now see the funds?"

"Soon, M. Moreau. Very soon. But first my financial advisor must examine the ring." Without waiting for permission, Dirk picks it up and hands it to Oliver. "Would you mind having a look at this?"

"With pleasure." Much to my surprise Oliver pulls out a jeweler's loupe and sticks it in his eye. He sees Olivia staring at him and says, "We have a bit of jewelry in the family. I learned how to assess quality."

It takes forever for him to examine the ring, and while we wait, I watch the boy, who's still sitting on the ground making a sandal. Dirk has moved so he's standing close to me, my hand is in my pocket, and my finger is twitching near the trigger. I'm supposed to slip the gun to him as soon as Oliver says, "This looks like a winner."

But instead of giving us the signal, Oliver takes the loupe out of his eye, puts in in his pocket, purses his lips and hands the ring to M. Moreau.

"I'm afraid this is not the Kettani Ruby. The stone is, indeed, a ruby, but it's of inferior quality and has several inclusions. The Kettani Ruby has none. And these stones surrounding it are not the flawless diamonds set in the Kettani ring.

M Moreau appears flabbergasted. "This has to be the Kettani Ruby. I was assured it was." He turns to Youssef. "You assured me it was. I paid you a large sum of money to bring me the real ring."

"I was told it was the real ring," Youssef yells. "How do you know these people are telling the truth? Perhaps they have changed their minds and are trying to get out of the agreement. I had no reason to doubt the person who sold it to me because he is close to the family."

M. Moreau whirls around to confront Dirk. "Is he right? Are you trying to get out of our deal? I've spent a great amount of money obtaining this ring for you. You must pay me."

Things are getting loud, and I'm getting scared. When Youssef makes a threatening move toward Dirk, my entire body tenses, including my finger on the trigger. Somehow the gun in my pocket goes off, and a bullet zings between the two men and lands in a piece of leather hanging on a wall. Youssef utters a stream of words in Arabic, which I'm guessing are extremely colorful, and the young boy runs out the back yelling something I can't understand, but will probably insure we're surrounded by angry souk merchants momentarily.

Confused, Youssef looks for the source of the shooting. Dirk has M. Moreau backed against a wall, so Youssef knocks me down as he lunges at Oliver. Olivia, not liking what she sees, sticks out her foot and trips Youssef, who splats on the ground. I shoot again, this time on purpose because I'm terrified, and the bullet goes high and hits shelves holding all kinds of leather pieces and sewing items. The shelf crashes to the ground, pinning Youssef under it. I scramble to my feet and grab Oliver's arm.

"I didn't kill him, did I? Please tell me I didn't. Can you go look, Oliver, and see if he's breathing. I don't want to go to a Moroccan jail."

Dirk is already helping Youssef to his feet. "Relax, Julia. He's fine. There isn't even any blood. I would, however, like to hear an explanation for all this."

Now I point to the door, which is filled with concerned young men.

"Tell them to go away, Youssef. All we want are a few minutes conversation, then we'll be out of here and you all can go back to doing…whatever."

Youssef yells at the crowd in the door, and whatever he said is effective because the men disperse. M. Moreau sits down at the table and rubs his bald head.

"I cannot understand how this could happen. I paid good money for that ring. It has to be the Kettani Ruby."

"Well, it's not," Dirk tells him. "Didn't you examine it before you paid for it?"

"I did. I was able to tell it was a ruby, so I thought it was authentic." He pulls out a handkerchief and wipes his forehead. "I have to confess to you I'm not a gem expert. I mostly deal in…let us say, estate items."

"You mean stolen items? Like the elephant pin you tried to sell me?" Dirk gives me a warning look, but I can't stay quiet. "Who gave you that pin to sell?"

"A man. I don't know if he was the owner. He simply asked me to sell it for a good price. He told me the elephant tusks on that pin were genuine ivory."

"Wrong again. I suggest you find another line of work, M. Moreau," I say.

Oliver picks up the ring and holds it up to the light. "You can almost see the inclusions this way. Someone went to a great deal of trouble duplicating the Kettani Ruby. It might actually have fooled someone." A flush spreads over M. Moreau's face, and Oliver says, "I don't mean you. I'm not trying to be unkind. I'm talking about someone who actually knows a good bit about gems. Do you have any idea who this could be?"

M. Moreau shakes his head. "Ever since word got out that the

Kettani Ruby was missing, many unscrupulous people have been trying to profit from rumors that it has been found or someone has it and is offering it for sale. I've seen other rings, but they're made of glass and easily recognized as fakes. This one—I was sure it was real. I paid a large sum for it because I thought I was going to earn an even greater amount from you."

I almost feel sorry for the distraught man. He's not a very smart crook.

"One more question and then we'll be on our way. "Someone gave this ring to Youssef to give to you. Who was it?"

All eyes swing to the sheep's head merchant. "It was the man in the goat house. He came by and said he had something extremely valuable and would need money before he would give it up. Youssef contacted M. Moreau, and the rest you know.

Ah ha! The man in the goat house is Jamal.

Curious men have quietly entered the stall and are listening to the conversation. We need to leave. I poke Dirk in the ribs. "Can we go? They don't have any more info. We can talk this over somewhere less crowded."

After repeated assurances from us that we're not calling the police, and our only interest was and still is the return of the Kettani Ruby, Youssef leads us out the back of the stall and down an alley to the Square. I don't relax until we're in a taxi on our way to La Mamounia.

On the way back to the hotel, I call Mal to give her the bad news about the ring. She accepts the news fatalistically. "We'll probably never find it," she says. "I'm giving up."

This reaction spurs me into action. We divert the taxi to the little village outside Marrakech in the hopes of finding and talking to Jamal. But he's gone. I know when we pull up on the dirt in front of the one-window house that we'll have no luck.

The door is open and as we peer into the dark interior, we realize it's empty. The old woman and little girl are also gone. The only sign of life is a cat that runs out between our legs and sits on a rock a few feet away. It hisses at us as we try to approach. So that's it. We leave Morocco tomorrow, and we didn't find the Kettani Ruby and we don't know who killed Abdul, and we have no more leads. I feel like I've let Mal and Suad down.

Chapter 27

Our last day in Morocco. Later this afternoon Olivia, Oliver, Dirk and I will fly to Paris, but now it's very early in the morning, and we're somewhere outside Marrakech in a field watching the sunrise. As a going-away surprise, Vivian has organized a hot air balloon ride for us and the nice folks we met on the Sahara trip. Balloon rides over Marrakech are a popular tourist activity, which Olivia will miss because she doesn't feel well and has stayed at the hotel. She'll meet us later at Mal's for a farewell brunch. And, since Paris is our ultimate destination today, I'm wearing what I hope will pass for French chic; blue pants, a lace top, my pendant from the souk, two bracelets, and a sparkly butterfly clip in my hair.

Balloon riding will probably not be my favorite thing to do, but who knows. I could have sworn camel riding wasn't either, but I'm glad I did it. Bobbing around in the air in a basket doesn't sound like fun, but I have to admit the colorful balloons waiting on the green grass are beautiful. As the sun comes up, the landscape glows in a warm light, and there isn't a cloud in the sky.

A smiling girl offers juice and pastry and tells us about the flights. "We have different kinds of rides. There are balloons for two people and four people. And please do not worry. This is very safe, and you will see wonderful things."

The three of us have already decided to go together on one of the big balloons, and as we watch, men are scurrying around checking things on a silver, pale green and rose balloon, which is the one we'll be using.

I adjust my sunglasses and say to anyone who's listening, "Isn't this exciting? This whole trip to Morocco has been quite an adventure, hasn't it? I mean, maybe not getting clonked on the head or assaulted in the souk, but otherwise, it's been an amazing experience. Wake Forest is going to be awfully tame after this." And as a non-sequitur, I add, "I don't know how these balloons get off the ground, although I used to say that about airplanes."

Oliver points to the red, purple, gold and green striped balloon next to us. "That thing at the top of the basket is the burner. The pilot lights it and fire heats the air in the balloon, which makes it lighter than air. That's what makes it rise. Then the pilot uses wind direction to steer it"

This sounds extremely random. We could end up anywhere. I wander away from our little group to look at the other balloons. I spot the Bouchers and greet them with my very fluent *Bon Jour.* They smile, say something, and I nod and pretend I understand.

There are probably fifteen to twenty balloons inflated and ready to go. I have to admit it's a beautiful sight. I walk until I come to the balloons for two people at the edge of the field and stop at a particularly pretty one that reminds me of cotton candy —pale pink swirls in clouds of color that look like marshmallows. It must be getting ready to leave because the pilot is already in the basket, and there's a man holding a rope to keep it from prematurely sailing away.

"Awesome, isn't it?"

I nearly jump out of my skin. Corey Fieldstone is standing so close to me I can feel his breath on my neck.

"You scared me, Corey. You shouldn't sneak up on people like that."

"Sorry, Julia. I didn't mean to scare you, but I'm glad to see you now. This will give us a chance to have a little talk."

"I'm afraid this isn't a good time, Corey. I have to get back to my friends." I back up because he's in my personal space, and I can smell his breath, which isn't pleasant. He reeks of sardines and garlic.

"Why are you so unfriendly? You were certainly eager to talk on the plane, but since then I've felt a certain antagonism."

I sigh. This is not the time to have this conversation, but I don't know how to get away from him, so I say, "It's like this, Corey. I'm sure you're a nice person, but you're trying too hard. Frankly, you're a bit annoying."

I figure this remark should end our chat, but it doesn't.

"Surely you have time for a short talk."

"I don't, and I can't imagine what we'd have to say to each other. I need to get back to my friends now."

I try to get past him, but he blocks my way and smirks. "I can think of several topics, such as what your snooping has uncovered. You've certainly been busy."

A tiny kernel of fear begins to gnaw at my stomach. "Please get out of my way," I say briskly with a bravado I don't feel.

"Afraid I can't do that, Julia." He steps aside and points to the door on the balloon basket. "Get in."

Excuse me? "Why on earth would I do that? I'm going in a bigger one with my friends."

"I don't think so. Like I said, get in."

I put my hands on my hips and glare at him. Honestly, this man is so annoying.

"Listen here, Corey. I don't know what you think you're doing, but you're sounding a little bit crazy. Now please get out of my way. Dirk will be missing me."

"You're so tiresome. Will this convince you?" He pulls a gun out of his pocket and points it at my heart. Now will you please get in. I'm asking nicely."

Now I'm terrified. This isn't good, which is an understatement. I consider my options. I don't know what's wrong with Corey, but I can't believe he'd be nuts enough to shoot me here. But as I look around, I realize we're almost alone. The balloon pilot has to see the gun, but he's busy lighting a cigarette and looking at the sky. The man holding the rope is sitting on the ground with his back to us. I could try to run, but he could shoot me and disappear in the woods next to the field before anyone sees me. I seem to have no other choice. I step into the balloon.

"So what are you doing, Corey? And do you have to wave that gun around?"

But Corey isn't listening to me. He wiggles the gun in the pilot's face, the pilot lights the burner and I hear the whoosh of fire. Then Corey points the gun at the guy with the rope and yells something in French. The guy drops the rope and takes off running. Before I know it, we're off the ground, and I'm holding the side of the basket for support. The pilot tries to surreptitiously use his cell phone, but Corey snatches it out of his hand and throws it over the side.

"Let's settle down now, folks," he says. "Julia, you and I need to chat."

"I have nothing to say to you, Corey, and I'm certainly not going to talk to you as long as you have that gun."

"Suit yourself. I'm afraid I'm going to keep it, though. Let's talk about the Kettani Ruby. I know you've been hunting for it."

"I'm confused. What's the Kettani Ruby to you? And where's your wife? Why isn't she on this little jaunt?" Actually, I'm not confused. I'm scared to death, and I can feel my heart thudding in my ears. Corey's behavior is so out of character and outrageous. I want to keep him talking until I can figure out what to do.

"I have no idea where she is, nor do I care."

"That's harsh, Corey." As we talk I look down and immediately feel dizzy. We're above the trees and bobbing erratically. I see our little group standing next to a balloon, and they obviously don't yet know I'm missing. "What are we doing, Corey? What do you want? I need to get on the ground because I'm feeling sick."

"Too bad, Julia. So tell me what you've found out about the ring."

"Nothing. And wait until Dirk hears about this. He doesn't like people threatening me."

Corey cackles. "I don't care about him, although he must be a strong dude if he could take down Jamal."

"You know Jamal?"

"I know everything. I owe a lot of money because of this ring, so I need for you to tell me where it is."

"I don't think the Kettanis are going to like hearing you've kidnapped me. They probably won't be inviting you to anymore social functions."

He makes a rude sound. "Why would I care about social functions?"

"Isn't that the reason you're always hanging around?"

"I was hanging around because I needed to be close when the ring was found."

This is a completely different Corey. He doesn't sound nearly as obsequious and fawning as he did.

"Well, for the millionth time, I don't know where the ring is. And if I did, I wouldn't tell you." That's a pretty bold statement considering I'm standing in a basket up in the sky and an idiot is pointing a gun at me. Talk, Julia, talk.

"How did you learn about the Kettani Ruby? Do they know about it in Pennsylvania or wherever you're from?"

He sneers. "So many questions. You've heard of social media, haven't you? When such an important piece goes missing, all kinds of things appear online. You have to know where to look."

"So you came all the way to Morocco to find it? That sounds improbable." When he doesn't answer, I say, "Here's another question. Were you the one who hit me on the head in the desert?"

He bows. "Guilty as charged. You know, Julia, you can be infuriating. I searched your tent and couldn't find anything, so I thought if I scared you enough, you'd come to me for protection since we were the only Americans on the trip. Then you'd spill your guts about all you know."

I stare at him in astonishment. "You've got to be kidding. I can promise you that would never happen." I notice his hand holding the gun has dropped to his side. Can I rush at him and take it away?

As if he can read my mind, his hand comes up, and he aims the gun at my stomach. "However, all this is not my immediate problem. As I said before, I've lost a good bit of money, and I intend to get it back."

I fold my arms across my stomach and look at the sky pretending to be bored.

"It happened this way. I heard a spoiled, wealthy and probably stupid American woman was willing to pay an outrageous sum for the Kettani Ruby. I contacted Jamal, who knew a jeweler who could make a copy of the ring. He obviously had to use real rubies and diamonds, so the price was significant. But the jeweler agreed to a small down payment with the promise of a large payment once the ring was sold. The ring was fabricated and delivered to me and I asked Youssef to contact the French jeweler, Monsieur Moreau, who would make the sale to the woman. M. Moreau honestly thought he was buying the real Kettani Ruby at a fabulously discounted price. Everyone else knew it was a fake. Moreau paid me a minimal down payment fort the ring with the promise of much more after the final sale. See where I'm going here. We're all out of money because the final sale didn't go through. I have to pay the man who made the ring, Jamal gets a cut because he found the jeweler. Youssef gets a cut because he found M. Moreau. I need my money from M. Moreau so I can pay the man who made the ring. Do you understand what I'm saying, Ms. Stephanie Orca Wesley? You're responsible for all our losses."

I don't know what to say. Corey has a network of crooks here in Marrakech? Fortunately I don't have to speak because he continues.

"This is how it's going to go down. I don't think you have much money, but I think your friends Dirk Harrison and Oliver Parker-Smythe do. As we speak, your best buddy, Olivia Duncan, is now—let us call it—under our protection. We will release her when we receive $1,000,000 in cash." His smile is evil. "We're being kind. This is less than the value of the Kettani Ruby."

I drop all pretense of being bored. "You've kidnapped Olivia? Are you crazy? You'll never get away with this. I swear, Corey, if anyone hurts her you'll regret it."

"It's already done." He pulls a paper out of his pocket. "Give this to your boyfriend when you see him. And don't try to call the police. Kadem Kettani doesn't like the law looking into his guests. Olivia will be fine as long as you do as you're told."

He says something to the pilot, and the balloon begins to slowly descend. I hang onto the side of the basket. “What are we doing, Corey?”

“We aren’t doing anything. You are getting out.”

I hold on tightly. “I’m not going to let you throw me overboard.”

“Relax, Julia. I’m not going to hurt you. I just want to say it hasn’t been a pleasure knowing you. Do as you’re told, and everything will be fine.”

I look over the side and see the ground growing closer and closer. Now my heart is thumping so wildly, I’m afraid I’m going to pass out.

“Once the basket hits the ground you’ll have to move fast,” Corey says. “You’re a resourceful woman so I’m sure you’ll be able to find your way back to your friends.”

The pilot tries to set the basket down gently, but it bounces on the ground a few times until Corey yells, “This is it. Get out!.” He opens the door and pushes me out. I land on my back on the ground and hear the burst of fire as the balloon rises above me.

Chapter 28

I have no idea where I am. The balloon came down in a clearing, but I'm surrounded by trees and there's no sign of life. My cell phone says no service. Thinking about Olivia being kidnapped makes me sick. I have to find a way to call Dirk and Oliver.

When I was up in the balloon, I saw a little village and now try to figure out where it could possibly be. Olivia always laughs at my sense of direction, which is horrible. I begin walking, hoping I'll find civilization soon.

As I walk, I think about Corey. It's clear to me he came to Morocco to find the Kettani Ruby. Was our meeting on the plane accidental? I try to remember how that happened. It was late at night, and I'd just left the bathroom. The plane lurched a bit, and I bumped into him as he was coming out of the galley. We both laughed and apologized, and when he said he couldn't sleep and did I want to join him for a glass of wine, I thought why not? Could he possibly have known I was going to the Kettani house in Marrakech? Who would have told him that? I honestly don't think he even knows Peter. He could have read about Nabil

Kettani in many financial publications. Or googled him. Or googled the whole Kettani family. These days you can find out anything about anyone.

How does he know Jamal and Youssef? This really puzzles me. He hasn't been here long enough to have made many connections. It doesn't make sense. I don't have answers. And I wish I could stop walking. My back hurts from falling on the ground, and now my feet hurt. What if I never come to any form of civilization? I suppose I'll die in the woods, and my flesh will be pecked off by ravens. That's a disgusting thought. Do they even have ravens in Morocco? Why am I thinking that? I need to stop thinking altogether. Fortunately, I reach a dirt road before I really go around the bend. There are tire tracks, which must lead to somewhere. A truck loaded with pigs chugs toward me, and I frantically wave my arms, but the driver doesn't stop. The truck veers around me stirring up a cloud of dust.

I walk until I think my feet are going to fall off. When I hear a car behind me, I think I'm probably hallucinating. It slows and stops next to me, and I debate diving into the woods. I want to be rescued but what if this is someone connected to Corey? I'm ready to scream as both car doors open, and men jump out. I can't believe my eyes when I see Dirk and Oliver. Dirk grabs me and pulls me into a hug. I'm so relieved, I could cry. They found me.

"Thank heavens for GPS on your phone. Do you have any idea how worried we've been? I almost had a heart attack when I heard you and Fieldstone were in a balloon, and he had a gun."

"Yeah, yeah," I say. "It was awful, but you have to listen. Corey said he's kidnapped Olivia."

I remember the paper in my pocket. "Here. It says if you want her back, you have to pay $1,000,000."

Dirk glances at the note and hands it to Oliver. "This guy is seriously not well. He wants us to leave the money in unmarked bills on a bench near the fountain on Kettani's property. When he receives the money, he'll have Olivia released. He must watch a lot of TV. This sounds like amateur hour."

Maybe," I say, "but I need to find Olivia. He's just crazy enough to do something bad."

Oliver pulls out his phone. "I think this guy is a loon. I'm going to call her, and I'm willing to bet she's still asleep. She's definitely not a morning person."

He puts the phone on speaker, and I hold my breath as I wait for her to pick up. But she doesn't. It goes to voice mail.

"This doesn't mean anything," he says. "She could be in the bathroom."

I point to the phone. "Try her again."

Still no answer.

"I'll call the front desk and ask someone to check her room," Oliver says. "This may make her mad if she's trying to sleep, but at least we'll know she's safe."

We wait an agonizingly long time, but finally a voice says, "I regret to tell you Ms. Duncan is not in her room, and there seems to have been some kind of a disturbance. A chair has been upended, and a vase with flowers was smashed on the floor." The voice becomes stern. "Ms. Duncan will be responsible for damages."

Oliver jams the phone in his pocket. "Let's go. We have to find Olivia and get her away from this crackpot." He strides to the car and yanks the door open.

Dirk and I hurry after him and climb into the car. "Where are we going? How do you know where he's keeping her?" I ask.

"I don't know, but I can't stay here doing nothing." In spite of the seriousness of the situation, it makes me happy to hear how much he cares about my friend.

Oliver pounds the steering wheel. "I swear I'm going to kill this &@#$%*! if he so much as touched a hair on her head. I think we should hunt for her in the souks. I'll tear them apart to find her. If this jerk knows Jamal or Youssef, he might have persuaded them to hide her in a stall."

As Oliver rages, I look at Dirk, who hasn't said much. "What are you thinking?"

He smiles. "You can read my mind. I've been thinking that I don't think Fieldstone would try to hide her in the souk—even if he does have friends to help him. She stands out as a foreigner, and a lot of people would see her. But what if he knows of an empty house, away from crowds, where he could stash her without being discovered? A place where people—even if they did see Fieldstone with a western woman—would keep their mouths shut?"

Oliver stops pounding the steering wheel and says, "You know of such a place?"

"I do!" I shout, "and you do, too. The house with one window!"

"That's the one," Dirk says. "I think it's worth checking out. If we don't find her there, we can always storm the souks."

Oliver wheels the car around and steps down on the gas, and the car roars down the road to the outskirts of Marrakech.

Oliver pulls the car onto the dirt and kills the engine. This morning the goats are there, munching on a scraggly, skinny tree. There's no other sign of life. I notice in daylight the lone window is heavily smudged with mud and debris.

Dirk gets out of the car and points to me. "You wait here. And watch out for Fieldstone in case he's lurking somewhere around here. If you see him, lay on the horn."

"There's no way I'm staying here. I'm coming with you."

Dirk wants to argue but looks at my face and realizes it would be useless. I take a deep breath, straighten my back and march to the door. It's still ajar, which I hope means there are no bad guys in there. He pushes it open and we go in. It's dark and cold, and the room smells of stale cigarette smoke.

We use our cellphone flashlights to look around. There's a straw mat on the floor and a table with an empty can of Pepsi and a crumpled McDonald's wrapper. And an ashtray full of cigarette butts.

"Someone's been here," I say. "And I don't think the person is Moroccan. This is American food."

It's not hard to see Olivia isn't here, and I know Oliver is upset because he's pacing around muttering to himself. I'm ready to leave. The idiot must have put her in one of the stalls in the souk. I'm at the door when I hear Dirk say, "Can you two come here a minute? I think I've found something. There's an opening to another space."

The opening is covered by a cloth and is about two feet square. We look through the hole and see it's empty except for a pile of what looks like old curtains against one wall.

Dirk pulls the fabric away. "I don't think Oliver and I will fit through this space, but you will, Julia. Will you go have a look?"

Reluctantly, I agree and crawl through, trying not to think about what could be slithering around in there. The area is too small to permit me to stand up straight, so I have to crouch as I try to walk. As I move about, I shine my flashlight on the dirt floor and ceiling. I mean, those snake charmers have to get their reptiles from somewhere, and I sure don't want one to fall on me from above—or tickle my ankles.

I stop at the heap of fabric and examine it closely. It is actually a pile of drapes and they're too clean to have been here long—an incongruous sight in this dirty hovel. I touch the pile with my toe and almost jump out of my skin when it moves. And makes a noise. I can't determine what kind of a noise, but it definitely doesn't sound like a snake or a rat. I scream, and the pile of cloth moves more.

Dirk sticks his head through the opening. "What's wrong, Julia? Are you hurt?"

"This pile is alive, and I'm not touching it. I have to get out of here."

Now I hear Oliver's voice. It's soft and reassuring, and I know he's trying to calm me down. "Try to lift off some of the fabric. I know you can do it."

"Not in this lifetime. Whatever is under here is solid and heavy. I'm coming out."

"I'm begging you, Julia. Pull the drapes off."

His voice is so urgent, I do as he asks and gingerly pick up a corner of the fabric and pull it off, only to reveal another underneath it. Even in the dark I can tell these are heavy damask drapes and wonder why anyone would put them in here. And the noise from somewhere in the pile is getting louder. It's a high pitched, keening sound that makes the hair stand up on the back of my neck, but I keep going. When my hand touches hair, I almost faint. I have my fingers on a rat. But a rat doesn't have thick long hair. And the head attached to the hair is shaking violently, throwing off more drapes. I summon all my courage and shine my flashlight on the pile. And am totally speechless.

I'm looking at a wild-eyed Olivia, with duct tape over her mouth and ropes around her hands and feet. I rip the tape off her mouth and release a stream of words that would make a sailor blush.

"That weasel, Brandon, did this. What a creep! Get me out of here. I want to find him and kill him."

Oliver is yelling to Olivia, Olivia is yelling at me, and no one can understand a word, but the relief is palpable. We found my best friend, and she's safe!

Oliver tosses me his pocket knife, and I saw through the ropes, free Olivia and quickly help her up. She alternates between hugging me and rubbing her wrists to start the circulation.

"Thank you a million times. How on earth did you find me? That jerk, Brandon, told me you'd crashed in a hot air balloon and were probably dead. That's why I went with him. He said he was going to take me to the crash site. Although when he first came to the room, he and I had a bit of a misunderstanding. I may have thrown a vase at him. By the way," she says as we approach the opening, "I heard you say I'm heavy."

"I meant the pile of drapes, Olivia. Not you," I say as I push her through. Lordy!

While Olivia and Oliver hug each other, I look around for Dirk, who's not in the room. I go outside and see him leading Brandon across the dirt to the house. I can't help noticing Dirk's captive is pretty compliant and wonder why—until I see Dirk poking a stick in Brandon's back. Dirk winks at me and puts a finger to his lips.

"I caught him trying to break into the car," Dirk says. "He doesn't want to tell me what he's doing here, but I figure he's one of Fieldstone's buddies."

I almost jump up and down in excitement. "He kidnapped Olivia, but she's okay. We found her in there," I tell him, pointing to the house.

"Good. We'll tie him up and tell Mal what we've done. It's up to her to call the police."

We had to restrain Olivia to keep her from pounding on Brandon. We didn't let her touch him, but I think the jerk understood her anger. We left him on the dirt floor with his hands and feet tied and the door open. He could call for help. It didn't matter now.

Chapter 29

"I can't believe Corey did that! I knew he had an ulterior motive for hanging around here, but I didn't think it was harming my friends." Ever since we arrived, Mal has been hanging onto us as if we'd disappear if she let go. "I'm just so sorry, Julia. I should never have let him in the house."

Dirk, Olivia, Mal and Oliver are sitting at the table in the kitchen of the Kettani residence, and Suad is plying them with amazing food and urging them to eat. I'm running now on nervous energy, and I'm afraid if I sit down, I'll pass out, so I shuffle around listening to them talk. Today has been exhausting, and Olivia amazes me. For someone recently tied up and covered with drapes, she's amazingly chipper. And hungry. She glances up as I pass her chair and she catches my look.

"What? If you'll recall, I missed breakfast."

I smile and cruise by Mal. "Here's a question that's been bothering me. Was my meeting with Corey on the plane accidental or did you tell him I was coming?"

"Julia! Of course I didn't tell him you were coming. I didn't even know him, and to be perfectly honest, I don't know who invited him to the party. I assumed he was some casual acquaintance of the family."

"Are the police looking for him now?"

She nods. "We didn't call them. Dirk did, and he must have been quite forceful because two officers came to the house to tell us they had squads of men out looking for him. They know where he landed, but it took a while for the pilot to return to the field because Corey disabled the balloon. So he had a head start."

It makes me shiver to think this maniac is on the loose, but I tell myself we don't have to worry. Soon we're flying to Paris, and we'll be far away from this chaos.

"What about Brandon?" I ask. "He and Corey were obviously working together. Who hired him to be the security person here?"

Mal frowns. "I'm pretty sure Vivian did. I think Corey recommended him. Vivian said she felt more secure with an English-speaking bodyguard, and you know how she felt about Corey. He probably sweet talked her into giving Brandon a job." She puts her fork down and stares out the window. "This was all a setup, wasn't it? Nothing was coincidental."

"It certainly looks that way. What has Vivian said about all this?"

Before she can answer, the devil herself sweeps into the kitchen. Vivian is wearing a long crimson robe, an anguished look on her face and is dabbing at her eyes with a handkerchief.

"Oh, girls! I am genuinely appalled at the events of this morning. How on earth could that nice Mr. Fieldstone do such a thing? I'm beside myself with remorse for bringing him into our home. He had us all fooled." She stops talking, wipes her nose delicately and looks at me. "Are you sure it was Mr. Fieldstone who accompanied you in the balloon? After all, it was early in the morning; perhaps the light wasn't sufficient to identify individuals…"

"What rubbish, Vivian," Mal retorts. "Of course, she knows who forced her into the balloon. It was indeed, that "nice Mr. Fieldstone."

"What can you tell us about Brandon?" I ask. "After all, he was in your employ."

"I know very little about him. I believe he was hired by Kadem. He knew how I needed to feel comfortable with the staff. I prefer someone who—how shall I say this?—understands how we live. In other words, one of us."

This remark makes five of us shudder. "So you didn't hire him?"

She gives me a cold look. "My dear, I don't hire staff. My concern now is about you and your friend. We are thankful you're both unharmed. You will be leaving Morocco today, yes?"

"Yes, we will. I was hoping to say goodbye to Kadem and Peter before we left."

"Ah, I'm afraid that won't be possible. They have extended their business trip."

Mal shakes her head. "Nope, that's wrong, Vivian. They're both on their way home. I'm surprised your husband didn't tell you. They won't be here before you guys leave, Julia, but I sure will tell them everything that's happened."

If looks could kill, we'd be mourning our good friend, Mal, who should have zipped her lips. I've had enough of Vivian, so when I see Suad standing at the sink, I go over to speak to her. "You eat now?" she asks worriedly. "You no hunger?"

"Yes, I no hunger. At least not right now." I reach into my bag and pull out a little gift for my favorite cook. It's a photo of the two of us that Olivia snapped in the kitchen. I've put it in a little frame and am hoping it makes Suad smile to look at it when we're gone. I hand it to her and say, "This is for you."

I'm astonished to see tears well up in her eyes. She clutches the photo with both hands and smiles. "Very good." And then a flood of words I don't understand but must be expressive because the other two ladies at the sink drop what they're doing and cluster around us. There's much head bobbing and smiling and pointing to the images in the photo. One lady looks up from the photo to glance at me and does a double take. She pokes the pendant I'm wearing.

"Abdul's"

Now I recognize her. It's Abdul's sister. I remember Mal telling me they'd hired her to help out in the kitchen.

"Abdul's," she says again. "Where you get?"

"In the souk." I'm confused. This belonged to Abdul? Why was it in the souk? And now his sister is visibly upset. She's crying and clutching the pendant.

The others hear the commotion and leave the table to join us, which is good because I need translation help. And I need the sister to let go of the pendant. She's pulling so hard I'm forced to follow her as she turns to show another lady the pendant. Now they're all chattering at once, and I have no idea what's happening. Suddenly Dirk holds up his hand, says something, and they all stop talking.

It seems to take forever but finally Dirk says, "It seems Abdul gave his sister a little box to keep for him. He told her to protect it, but she looked at the contents and decided they might bring a little money, so she took them to the souk to sell. She said there wasn't anything of major value, so she didn't understand why Abdul was so adamant about keeping the box safe. Then her other brother, the shaman, told her she shouldn't have done that and that he'd given a key to an American lady. I think that means you, Julia. Didn't you go see a shaman?"

I'm more confused than ever. "I did go there, but I don't

have a key."

"But he did give you something," Olivia interrupts. "It was that strange little pin."

Dirk points to the pendant. "Would you mind letting me see that, Julia?"

I take it off and hand it to him. "I don't understand why you want to see it. I'm pretty sure the stone is glass, and the 'gold' chain is turning my neck green."

He weighs it in his hand. "It feels a bit heavy for what it's supposed to be."

"That's why I bought it," I tell him. "It seemed more substantial than the usual junk."

"May I see that?" Oliver already has his jewelry loupe in his eye and inspects the trinket.

I nudge Olivia. "Does he have that with him all the time?"

She, however, ignores me. "Where's that thing the shaman gave us?"

Before I can answer, Oliver points to the bottom of the pendant and says, "There's a tiny opening here." He looks at me. "Did Abdul's brother give you something that resembles a pin? That could be the key he was talking about."

"I repeat, Julia," Olivia says. "What did you do with it?"

Lordy! I think I put it in my purse, but not the purse I have with me today. The other purse, which is packed in my suitcase and is in the trunk of the car. Dirk and I go out to the car, pull out the suitcase and open it. The purse is, naturally, on the bottom. I find it, though, and carry it back into the house. They all crowd around me as I open it and dump out the contents. For a minute I'm afraid the little pin isn't there. Could I have thrown it out? I honestly never thought we'd need it for anything. But I spot the plastic baggie hiding under my bronzing moisturizer and breath mints. And the little pin thingy is still in there.

I hand it to Oliver, who sticks it in the hole on the end of the pendant. "It fits," he says, "but nothing happens."

I make an unladylike sound. "What did you expect to happen? I think we're all experiencing some kind of mass hysteria here. That pendant in your hand is a cheap trinket, and the pin thing is probably nothing."

Oliver isn't listening to me. His head is bowed over the pendant and his forehead is creased in concentration. "My fingers are too big for this." He hands the pendant and pin to me. "Can you try this, Julia? It wants to turn, but I can't get a firm grip."

I hold the pin between thumb and forefinger and insert it into the hole. It surprises me how easily it fits. I turn it to the right, and there's a collective gasp as the pendant opens, and I'm holding two halves of the trinket in my hand.

And in one half is the most beautiful, gorgeous, stunning ring I've even seen. Even in the dim kitchen light, the ruby glows a deep red, and the diamonds surrounding it flash patterns on the wall. I can't believe it, but I know I'm finally holding the famed and fabulous Kettani Ruby in my hand.

We are all stunned into silence. Finally, Olivia speaks. "You've been wearing this the whole time. Remember when it fell out of your bag in the tent and we found it under the bed? It was covered in sand. And when you put it in Mal's bag, and forgot about it? And when the clasp broke, and it fell in the toilet? How have you been keeping it closed, by the way?"

"A bit of dental floss. It sounds primitive, but it works."

"I have to sit down," Mal says. "My knees are wobbly."

Oliver carefully lifts the ring out of the pendant. "This is an amazing piece of jewelry. It makes me weak to think about… ah…what it has recently experienced. Thank heavens we have it now."

Vivian pushes Mal aside to look at the ring. "This is most excellent. I'm extremely relieved to have it returned. Are you sure this is the real Kettani Ruby? I understand there may have been other copies."

Oliver nods. "This is the genuine ring. I was able to see the tiny F engraved in the platinum band. And the ruby is flawless."

Vivian's smile reminds me of a shark about to devour something tasty. "If you wouldn't mind handing it to me, Lord Parker-Smythe, I'll make sure it's securely stored in a vault."

As she reaches for the ring, Mal snatches it out of Oliver's hand.

"Nice try, but he's not giving it to you, Vivian. Fatima told me she didn't want you to have it. It belongs to Peter."

"You have become very tiresome, Malika, and may I add, extremely ungrateful. I've done my best to welcome you into the family and to assist you with social duties, but you continually resist my efforts. I'm sure Kadem will have something to say about your stubbornness. Now please give me the ring. We are wasting time here. I'm the legal spouse of Kadem Kettani and the ruby belongs to me."

Mal sticks the ring down the front of her shirt and crosses her arms.

"Come and get it, you old witch."

Vivian tries to lunge at Mal, but I grab her by the arm and pull her away. She's about to take a swing at me when there are two loud bangs, which nearly scare the socks off us, and bullets fly into the wall behind us.

"Let her go or I'll shoot you all. I hope you can see I'm not fooling around."

Corey Fieldstone has come in the back door and has a large gun trained on us. He walks over to Vivian and says, "Are you okay, sweetheart?"

"Sweetheart?" five of us say in unison. "You call her sweetheart?"

"I sure do. She's my wife."

Chapter 30

Now I seriously have to sit down. Vivian and Corey are married? Isn't she already married to Kadem? Mal says what I'm thinking.

"She can't be your wife. She's married to my father-in-law."

He dismisses this fact with a wave of his gun. "She can't be married to him if she's legally married to me. And we were married first. It won't matter when we get back to the States. No one will know about this little adventure."

"Kadem will know," Mal says. "You won't get away with this. He'll find you."

Vivian sneers. "How will he do that? He won't know our real names, and the Kettani ruby ring will be a thing of the past. Corey, as you call him, has people lined up to take the ring apart. The ruby is already promised to a buyer. Kadem will never see the ring or us again."

"I can't understand this," I say. "Haven't you had a good life here, Vivian? Are you saying you don't love Kadem?"

"Bah! You're really slow to catch on and, you all are very dull. I never intended to stick around. Incidentally, Malika, I found a letter your precious mother-in-law wrote to you before she died. She never had a chance to mail it. It said she'd given the ring to Abdul to hide, and she wanted you to get it back and give it to Peter. It seems she was afraid I'd get it. Ironic, isn't it."

"Does anyone else notice her accent is slipping?" I ask.

Oliver nods. "I wondered why she didn't sound like she was from the Cotswold."

"So you're not from England?" I ask.

"I'm from the good old USA. We've been planning this for a long time. First, marry the old man. Then take the Kettani Ruby. You can probably understand how upset we were to hear the ring was missing. I had to go to so much trouble establishing myself as a Brit. When we read Kadem was attending a charity function in London, I flew over and pretended I'd come from the Cotswold. We met, I lit the fire of passion and I had to keep fanning the flames until he married me. That was tiresome."

I'm still confused. "So where is Bella?

Now Corey looks confused. "Who?"

"Bella, your wife. The person you brought to the desert."

He shrugs his shoulders. "I have no idea. I don't even know her last name, and I'm certainly not married to her. And I'm fairly certain her name isn't Bella. She's a friend of Jamal's and works in the souk. I needed a wife for social purposes, so she agreed to pretend to be married to me—for money, of course."

Vivian glares at her husband. "We did, however, run into some problems. We were doing okay until he decided not to wait for the ultimate payoff. He thought if he had a copy of the ring made, he could pass it off as the real thing to an unsuspecting, naïve buyer. When M. Moreau told Youssef about Stephanie Orca Wesley…well, you know the rest. My husband had already paid for an inferior ruby and needed to sell the fake ring quickly. Thanks to your snooping, things began to spiral out of control.

Ugh! This is sickening. "And the flight from JFK to Casablanca? Was our meeting also a setup?"

Vivian smirks. "Sure was. Your girlfriend here couldn't wait to give us all the details. She was so excited you and Olivia were coming, she even told me the flight number. It's a good thing you like wine. You made it easy for us."

"But we never talked about the Kettanis on the plane," I protest.

"No, you didn't, but I was able to put him on the guest list for the party by telling Malika he was a friend of yours, Julia. Your best buddy would do anything for you. After that it was easy. He needed access to the house."

I'm feeling dumber by the minute. "And Brandon?"

She frowns. "A mistake. Highly incompetent." She hooks a thumb at her husband. "He met Brandon in a hotel bar and unwisely decided he would be a great bodyguard. He actually gave me the creeps the way he prowled around the house. I'm sure he stole things. I know he tore up the living room in a drunken rage. We had to pretend we had a break in."

I'm afraid to ask the next question. I look at Corey. "Did you kill Abdul?"

"Nope, I didn't." He nods at Vivian. "She did."

I'm so shocked I can hardly speak, but Vivian is completely unremorseful. "I had to do it, you see. The ring disappeared about two months ago, and, although there were rumors, no one had any precise information about its whereabouts. And then right before you two arrived, I found the letter from Fatima. Well, naturally the only thing I could do was confront Abdul and demand he give it to me. I mean, after all I am a Kettani. The ring rightfully belongs to me." She picks a piece of lint off her jacket. "Unfortunately, he refused. I took the knife from the kitchen intending to scare him, but… you know the rest. So you see, my darlings, I've killed once for the Kettani Ruby. I'll certainly do it again."

I shake my head. "You are one sick puppy."

"Don't say that," she snarls. "Don't ever say that again."

"I'm curious, Vivian. Did you wash off in the fountain after you killed him? You must have been covered in blood."

"It was, indeed, messy. I found that idiot Brandon's jacket on a bench and tore off a piece to use as a rag. I actually thought that was a good plan. If anyone found the cloth in the fountain, perhaps Brandon would be accused of murder. I really had to hustle, too, because I knew we had to greet you two at some point. I barely had time to get the blood out of my fingernails."

I stand by my statement that she is a very sick puppy.

Corey, or whatever his name is, points the gun at me. "Okay, folks. Enough of the pleasantries. If you don't want to see this highly annoying person shot, I suggest you tell your friend here to pluck the ring out of her shirt and give it to me. Or I'll do it for her."

Dirk and Oliver don't like what they hear and move toward Corey. Corey, probably rattled at the sight of two strong men about to overwhelm him, backs up and fires wildly. The bullet hits a small chandelier hanging from the ceiling and thousands of expensive crystal shards cascade to the floor.

Corey regains his balance and this time trains the gun on Mal. "I've had it," he growls. "You have exactly one second to tell her to give me the ring."

Behind him I see Suad move from where she and Abdul's sister have been huddled, and she's holding a heavy frying pan. She sneaks up on Corey, swings and clonks him on the head. He goes down, and the men immediately grab him. Vivian springs to her feet and runs to Corey, but I intercept her and push her to the ground. For a scrawny woman she's extremely strong, and I have to straddle her to keep her on the floor.

"Someone help me here! She's bucking like a bronco."

Abdul's sister first spits on Vivian, then pulls a tieback off the curtains and hands it to Oliver, who uses it to tie the evil stepmother up. Suad hands Dirk another tieback and soon Vivian and Corey are firmly tethered to chairs. Both are complaining loudly. Dirk points the gun at them and says, "You know what, guys? I think we all are tired of listening to you. Either be quiet or I'm going to stuff dishtowels in your mouths." Thankfully, that worked.

Mal called the police and now we all stand around the kitchen waiting for them to arrive. Suad finds a broom and begins to clean up the broken pieces of chandelier, but Mal puts an arm around her and tells her to forget it.

Suddenly I remember something. "Suad, where did you put it?" When she looks at me in bewilderment, I make a stabbing motion in the air. Crude, but she understands. She opens a cabinet, pulls out a pile of clean towels and puts them on the floor, then reaches in and retrieves a plastic bag taped to the back. Holding it between thumb and forefinger she gives it to Dirk. The knife is plainly visible through the plastic. When Vivian sees it she turns a sickly shade of white, which makes her guilty of murder in my book.

Mal gasps. "What is that, Suad? Is that the knife that killed Abdul? Where did you get it?"

"It's a really long story, Mal, but you should thank Suad," I say. "I'm sure this knife has DNA on it which will prove Vivian killed Abdul."

Mal hugs Suad. "I am terribly grateful, and I can't wait to hear the rest of the story."

She pulls the ring out of her shirt and holds it in the palm of her hand. "This is beautiful, but it sure has caused a lot of trouble.

I'm going to give it to Peter when he gets home. He and Kadem can sort it out, but I never want to see it again."

"I certainly agree with you," I say. "This has been an amazing adventure, and I'm so happy the Kettani Ruby is back where it belongs. However, now I could use a bit of wine. My nerves are twanging like banjo strings. Anyone else with me?"

Mal grins. "This sounds really silly, but you know what I would like right now? A big piece of key lime pie!"

Lordy!

Four Months Later

I'm standing in front of the mirror in my bedroom trying to make my hair behave. I really want to look nice because Olivia and I are meeting Dirk and Oliver at the Raleigh airport in two hours. We're all going to Kill Devil Hills for a week of sun, ocean and relaxation.

Dirk and I haven't seen each other since the Morocco trip. We've both been busy. He had an important trial, and Olivia and I are building an addition onto Little Bites. We've also added amazing photos to our wall; pictures of the Blue Lagoon and a volcano in Iceland, wonderful photos of an eagle flying with a fish in his mouth from Alaska, and a sunny sand and sea scene from Hilton Head Island that makes you want to go there immediately. And, of course, photos of the Jemaa el Fna and the colorful, crowded souks in Marrakech. Our customers love them.

Every time I look at the photos of Morocco, I think about the Kettanis. Vivian Kettani, or Darlene Platt, as the Law refers to her, is in a Moroccan jail. Harold Platt, aka Corey Fieldstone, is, too. That can't be pleasant.

The Platts lived in Scranton, PA where Vivian/Darlene was manager of a fast food restaurant and an ardent admirer of all things British. She often spoke to her customers using an English accent and regaled them with stories of watching the royal weddings. Her hobby was reading about rich people in foreign countries. She's the one who told her husband about the Kettani Ruby, and she's the one who came up with a scheme to steal it.

Corey/Harold was an exterminator. His hobbies were bowling and reading true crime magazines. He usually did what his wife told him to do. They both dreamed of hitting it rich someday.

The police rounded up Jamal, Brandon, and Youssef. Jamal and Brandon are guests of the Moroccan judicial system. Youssef is still selling sheeps' heads because he apparently didn't commit any crime. M. Moreau is back home in France, hopefully a wiser man.

Kadem divorced Vivian/Darlene and has already moved on with a lady lawyer from Casablanca. From what Suad tells me, she's a lovely lady.

The Kettani Ruby is in a vault in a bank. Mal and Peter didn't want it, and the shaman, Abdul's brother, said it's cursed. Kadem tried to sell it, but no one wanted to deal with the curse. Apparently, folks with lots of money are superstitious.

Suad is still in the Kettani household, and she is happy. She occasionally cooks one of her fabulous meals but doesn't have much free time because she's now in charge of the entire staff. She assured me she has taught Abdul's sister everything she knows. She also gave me the recipe for her chicken and eggplant tajine, and we serve it at Little Bites. I brought a colorful tagine home with me, and when I carry it out of the kitchen—full of delicious food—the customers actually applaud.

So the bad guys are in jail, and life goes on. Now Olivia comes into my room carrying Boodles, the small terror that came to live with me after our Hilton Head adventure.

"He just peed on the rug in the living room, but I cleaned it up."

"Thank you. I don't know why that dog refuses to use the outdoor facilities."

Olivia moves next to me and applies more lip gloss. "I'm so excited! Aren't you? We should get going."

We hear the front door open and a voice call, "Let's go! They're going to land soon."

Mal bursts into the bedroom with Bubba, my English springer spaniel at her heels. "Are you guys ready? Peter's waiting in the car."

Yes, that's right. Mal and Peter live here now. They moved here two months ago and have a nice house in North Raleigh, just a few minutes from Wake Forest. Peter is finally using his law degree and is with a law firm in Raleigh. Mal is teaching part time at UNC. They have a rescue puppy of unknown ancestry named Rosie, in honor of the beautiful flowers in Marrakech. Rosie sleeps on their bed. They are happy.

I imagine we'll talk about Marrakech this week as we're enjoying the sun. I'm so thankful to be back home with the people I love. It was an amazing, exciting, scary time, and the best part of it was returning to the USA.

I touch the scar on my forehead, a permanent reminder of the trip. Would I do it again? Maybe. Not right now. But who knows what new adventure is just around the corner.

About the Author

Linda S. Clayton has been writing ever since she could hold a pencil. She wrote a poem for *Jack and Jill*, class songs, a college class play, *The History of Hair*—a book about her sister's many glorious hair colors and styles, and many other mostly forgettable things.

During the thirty years she and her husband lived overseas, Linda had a successful career as a portrait painter, but she never stopped writing. She wrote a humor column for an English publication in Bonn, Germany, and wrote countless attempts at novels that were shoved in the back of a drawer.

Her adventures and misadventures in foreign countries are providing a steady supply of material for her Julia Greene travel mysteries. The other books in the series are *An Ice Way to Die*, *A Killer of a Cruise*, and *The Little Bookstore Murder*.

Linda loves to grow vegetables—particularly tomatoes, travel and play with her two dogs.

www.ingramcontent.com/pod-product-compliance
Lightning Source LLC
LaVergne TN
LVHW091051080826
845145LV00002B/704